Havana Thursdays

» A Novel «

Virgil Suárez

Arte Público Press
Houston, Texas
1995

This volume is made possible through grants from the National Endowment for the Arts (a federal agency) and the Andrew W. Mellon Foundation.

Recovering the past, creating the future

Arte Público Press
University of Houston
Houston, Texas 77204-2090

Cover design by Gladys Ramirez
Original painting, "Introspections," by Nivia Gonzalez

Suárez, Virgil, 1962–
    Havana Thursdays / by Virgil Suárez.
       p.   cm.
    ISBN 1-55885-143-7 (clothbound)
    1. Cuban-American families—Fiction. 2. Cuban-American women—Fiction. 3. Cuban Americans—Fiction. I. Title.
    PS3569.U18H38   1995
    813'.54—dc20   95-9768
                                       CIP

For My Wife & Daughters
& the Alcázar-Poey Women
Who Inspired the Book

꿍

Havana Thursdays

৵৽

Characters

The Sisters

Laura

Maura

Their Daughters

Sofía

Beatriz

Cristina

Celia (Maura's)

The Sister's Mother-in-Law

Eleonor

Laura's Daughter-in-Law

Gisell

The Husbands, Son, & Boyfriends

Zacarías (Laura's Husband)

Norberto (Maura's Husband, Zacarías's Twin Brother)

Samuel (Laura's Son, Gisell's Husband)

Ariel (Sofía's Husband)

Lorenzo (Beatriz's Boyfriend)

Rafael (Celia's Boyfriend)

Also

Friends

Lovers

& Other Minor Characters

As They Appear

Primera

Dawn

1

Man Alone

The loud screech of a tropical bird awoke Zacarías before dawn. Inside the hut the darkness prevailed. Having forgotten that he was sleeping on a hammock, he tried to turn over on his side, but found it impossible. At that moment he remembered where he was: in the small farming village of Latinia, Brazil, less than twenty-five miles outside of São Paulo.

In the darkness of the hut, he sighed and grew still, as if waiting for the bird to cry out again, but he heard nothing. A dream, he thought, he was having a bad dream. And since he had overstuffed himself with *feijoada*, which the camp cook made for supper last evening, he realized it was possible that such heavy food caused the dream, the content of which he couldn't recall.

He suffered from severe heartburn and gas. Feasting on so much of the black beans with bits of pork and dried beef and deep-fried cassava wasn't good for him, he knew. All that fat and cholesterol. Can't be choosy so far away from the simple pleasures and comforts of hotels found in the bigger cities.

In the dark he brought his watch closer to his eyes and pushed the light button. The small screen of his digital, water-resistant watch (a Christmas gift from his wife Laura) lit up the time: 4 a.m.

One more hour and he and the workers, most of them *cablocos*, would have to return to the corn field. Today was Thursday, and he was overseeing the planting of a new line of hybrid corn seed which he himself had established. The seed

came from his test fields in Homestead, Florida, a city not too
far from Kendall where he lived.

He was short of breath.

"*Maestro*," a voice came from the deep dark of the hut.
"*¿Está despierto?*" It was Juan Carlos, his assistant, asking
whether he was awake.

He was not a *maestro*; he was a Ph. D. in seed genetics
with a specialization in corn, but he didn't mind being called
maestro. The connotation was that of teacher, one who was an
expert in his field, which he was. More than that, he *was* the
best corn-seed geneticist, which was why he was here in
Brazil, sent down by AID and the State Department.

"*Maestro...*"

"I'm awake, Juan Carlos," he said and cleared his throat.

Outside the men were already moving about, talking, getting ready for coffee and breakfast, perhaps a little restless
because they knew Sunday, their day off, was only three days
away. These were the best, the strongest, and the most ener-
getic men he had ever worked with, so he figured that every
minute of their leisure time together counted. Time relished.

"Are you all right?" Juan Carlos asked.

"Of course," he answered. "Why do you ask?"

"Your sleep was troubled," Juan Carlos said. "You spent
the night mumbling. Screamed once."

Was it he who had made the bird-like cry? "I am sorry if I
kept you awake."

"Not at all," Juan Carlos said.

He would have bet Juan Carlos was a sound sleeper, the
type who needed an explosion to go off by his pillow instead of
an alarm.

They made a good team, he and Juan Carlos. Laura
called them both workaholics who couldn't get enough of their
campos. Their fields. But theirs was only a working relationship, otherwise he might have told Juan Carlos that he,
Zacarías, slept poorly whenever he found himself away from
the warmth of his wife's body.

Zacarías thought of Laura for what seemed like a long time.

"Sun's coming out," Juan Carlos said.

Zacarías returned to a beautiful morning in the making. Already the smell of earth dominated the air, air which he breathed hard and deep. The dawn. He loved the fertile scent of moist dirt.

"Time to return to the field," he told Juan Carlos.

"We are making good progress," Juan Carlos said, and yawned. Being a soil-and-land-use engineer, he was overseeing the planting.

They had planted several acres so far, but they were far from done. All that planting in two days, Zacarías thought as he sat up on the hammock, wasn't bad. His feet and legs ached from standing all day in his work boots. Moving right along, he thought, and with his hands scrubbed his face, scratched the stubble on his cheeks and jaw. He stared at Juan Carlos moving about in the diluting dark of the hut, dressing. Zacarías was jealous of the young man's energy.

Outside, daylight bled a gray wash upon the hills surrounding the fields in the valley. The sun came up over the corrugated tin huts and small houses of woven branches, plaster and mud, stone and mortar, stucco and lime. The greens of the valley began to brighten.

Now the roosters in the distant backyards crowed.

"I will bring you some coffee," Juan Carlos said.

"Put a little water in it," he said. "The cook makes the *café* too strong."

Juan Carlos, dressed in beige khaki pants and calf-high boots, slid the curtain at the entrance so light flooded the hut. He walked out.

Sleeping inside the hut was okay, Zacarías thought, but he would never get used to hammocks, heat and the mosquitoes. How the workers lived with these inconveniences confounded him. The heat and mosquitoes. Juan Carlos knew of a way, by using smoke, of driving the mosquitoes out. This hut had two screened windows which would allow the air to circulate and keep the place cool.

The light of dawn showed the cracks on the dirt floor, whole ramifications of them. The workers' voices floated inside the hut as a distant murmur.

Castello, the camp manager and an old friend of Zacarías from back when Zacarías's father was alive, brought in a pail of water with which the *maestro* could wash his face and shave. "*Bom dia*," Castello said, and set the water on a fruit crate by the hammock.

"*Bom dia*, Castello," he greeted the short, robust man. "*Obrigado*."

The Portuguese Zacarías knew he learned years ago when he travelled with his father throughout Brazil. His father wanted him to learn the ropes so to speak, for him to see what a marvelous territory one day he too would have to work, either selling seed or planting. Brazil was his father's favorite country. Papi Torres, as Zacarías's father was called, knew its people and its history. For Papi Torres, Brazil was an exotic and enchanting place, a far away tropical paradise.

His father, Zacarías remembered, was, in a strange and enigmatic way, respected and admired, not so much because of what he knew about the land or what he had taught himself about the people and their language, but because of his looks. Both father and son stood out in this dark and rich land, being six-feet tall, blond, and green-eyed. Zacarías, however, liked to think that it was because of his amiable and jovial nature that these men were attracted to him.

Castello told Zacarías he hoped the rain stayed away from the area for at least the coming week; after that the rain would be good for the crop.

"The rain is our friend," Zacarías said. "It knows when to stay away.

Castello smiled.

"It also knows when we need it," Zacarías added.

"The rain is a godsend most of the time," said Castello. "I hate to sound ungrateful, but it could also be nothing but trouble when we are planting."

"If it rains," Zacarías said, "it'll remind us all of when we were children and played in it."

Castello nodded as if the memory took him back to his own childhood.

One of the men called out to Castello to step outside. Castello excused himself and went out.

Zacarías sat up in the hammock, grabbed his boots and slipped his feet into them. The leather of his boots was the color of the dirt and riddled with as many cracks and lines. He stood and approached the pail of water. Then as he bent over to wash his face, his chest muscles went into a spasm. A tightening. The recoiling started at the sternum and pulled inward.

Now he felt a severe pain cut through his chest. Quickly he sat back down on the hammock and clutched his heart as if to tear out the pain. The pain, becoming acute, jabbed at his heart under his ribs.

With whatever energy he could muster, he called out to Juan Carlos, or Castello, or somebody to come help him, for it rapidly became clear to him that he was having a heart attack.

A heart attack at his age. He couldn't believe it. Not at fifty-nine.

Several men, Juan Carlos among them, rushed into the hut when they heard his scream.

Juan Carlos, after the *maestro* told him the details of the pain, recognized the symptoms. But there was nothing he could do, having never learned the proper first-aid procedures to help in such emergencies. All Juan Carlos could do was make sure Zacarías was comfortable.

On his back Zacarías looked helpless and defeated, his six-foot frame too large for the small hammock. Juan Carlos placed a pillow under the *maestro's* head. Zacarías's blondish curls stuck to his sweaty temples and forehead. His once vibrant green eyes seemed to fade against his sunburnt face.

Juan Carlos told Castello to get on the radio and call São Paulo for an emergency helicopter.

Castello hurried out of the tent and ran to the jeep where he found the radio and called the city. In all the years working on the farmsteads, he had never seen a man have a heart attack, a young, healthy-looking man. Sure, he had seen plenty of people die before—shot after a bar brawl, or from being thrown off a horse, or his sister-in-law from giving birth—but not from a heart attack. The human body worked in strange ways.

It took a while to make the connection, but São Paulo quickly confirmed the immediate departure of the emergency unit.

Back in the hut Juan Carlos sweated profusely, feeling helpless, not knowing what to do. This situation was too scary for him.

Having trouble breathing, expecting the worst, Zacarías succumbed to the pain in his heart. He closed his eyes. He tried to swallow, but his throat had become parched. Right before Zacarías drifted away, the image of his lovely wife appeared in his mind. Laura, the mother of his children...

Laura!

❧

Segunda

Morning–Afternoon

2

A Different Thursday

It was one of those windy days when the gusts swept up leaves and debris into whirls, when it didn't make any sense to Laura to have the pool cleaned. It was a cloudy Thursday morning, and the tall masculine blond woman from Amazon Pool Cleaners came and went, and in spite of her brushing the bottom and dragging the net over the surface, the dirt and drowned insects once again speckled the water.

Never ending, Laura thought. Such was the nature of certain things.

She took a shower and got dressed in her favorite lavender blouse. The color, along with her black hair and black eyes, brought to her the drama she wished her life possessed whenever Zacarías was away on one of his long trips. He was far away and she was alone, and this morning she'd gotten up in a very quiet and peaceful mood.

She put a little mascara on, and while she did so, she sang "*Sabor A Mí*," Zacarías's favorite song and the one that capriciously surfaced in her mind.

Her voice was tender and resonant, still pretty good even though she had stopped singing a long time ago, even though these days she smoked too much.

In the bathroom mirror she made up her face, combed her hair and decided to wear it in a bun, held in place by a yellow scarf.

Now she craved a cup of coffee, so she put her shoes on and went to the kitchen. Waiting for the coffee to brew, she stood by the kitchen window and smoked one of her Benson & Hedges.

Laura stared out beyond the pool at the emptiness of the backyard. By the cinder-block fence that kept out the noises and traffic of the congested Kendall Drive, a wild-eyed opossum, a female, belly sagging with milk, scurried behind the ferns. What an ugly animal, she thought.

In the garden's lush greens (Zacarías had done a marvelous job with the garden and the landscape), the opossum stopped to smell the air and sniff over something dead on the wet grass. It looked up, saw the woman behind the glass of the kitchen window, then cut across the yard to her litter under the house next door.

What did they eat? Insects, worms, baby birds fallen from the nests high up on the palm trees, other smaller rodents? Laura shuddered.

Laura turned from the view when the coffee maker stopped brewing. She looked at the time on the oven clock where she had written herself a note stuck by the temperature knob as a reminder to broil a side of Honduran beef Zacarías had brought two weeks ago. Honduran beef *au jus*, the way the children liked it. She poured herself a cup of coffee and stirred in a teaspoon of sugar.

She removed the beef which was already defrosted out of the refrigerator and put it on the counter. She would prepare it and let it marinate all afternoon.

For some reason she felt tired even though by now she had had her dose of nicotine and caffeine. She hadn't been sleeping well. Whenever Zacarías was away, she had to contend with all that space on the bed. It felt unnatural to her, to have to sleep alone so often. She figured she'd never get used to his frequent and long absences.

What would he do when he had to retire? This was something she thought about quite often. Then, she would have him back in the house to stay. They would spend a lot of time together, get to know each other all over again. In that sense, she couldn't help but feel like a romantic.

If only her children were here. Why did she refer to her son and three daughters, and also her niece and godchild, as *the children*? They were no longer that. All are grown up now, with lives of their own. She remembered where they were this time of the day: Samuel was in Maryland, at the office; Sofía lived in Buenos Aires, Argentina; Beatriz was visiting her fiance in Mexico City; Cristina was on the road to Texas (she hadn't called to say of her exact whereabouts or how long it would take her to reach Corpus Christi); and her niece, the only one in town, taught at a high school in Homestead.

So, for whom was she cooking the beef? She was thinking of inviting her sister Maura and some of their friends for an early dinner. Today was Thursday, and she thought it would do Maura some good to get out of the house, now that Norberto was away at a conference in Mississippi.

Days like today she pretended she had her family back at the house, reunited for dinner.

Her routines had become ones of boredom. She got up, bathed, thought of places to go, things to do, people she wanted to visit, wrote letters to her daughter Sofía (she hadn't answered Sofía's last letter of distress), and sometimes napped or read in the afternoon. She read not only *Architectural Digest*, *Metropolitan Home,* and *Time* magazines, but thick books, the kind she knew would take her days to finish, and which she often didn't finish. If a book like *Corazón de Piedra Verde*, which she started to read the day Zacarías left, slowed in pace, she put it down and read Agatha Christie or one of those paperbacks by Le Carré or Clancy that Zacarías loved.

The house, though sparsely furnished and roomy, had always been a challenge to keep clean and with the perfect lived-in, cozy look. She had finally gotten all the colors right in each of the rooms. The living room was painted in pastel earth tones, Santa Fé style, and decorated with wicker and hand-painted pine furniture. The Florida room was Navajo white, with a solid blue sofa and a blue-flower pattern easy chair. This had been her mother's chair, which they had moved from Mexico City.

The kitchen, where she drank more coffee and smoked another cigarette, had Mexican tiles on the floor and pottery and handcrafts on the walls. There were plants too, which she watered every other day.

Sure, she had the help of the cleaning woman, but Rosana only came once every two weeks. Also, now that the children were not around as much, the house stayed clean longer. Yet dust always snuck inside the house, and somehow it managed to settle over everything, including the window sills and the top of the refrigerator. No doubt the wind brought it in, especially on days like this.

Should she call her sister Maura and ask her to come over early? Whether their husbands or any of their children were around, she and Maura kept the tradition of the family dinner alive. Every Thursday night they had dinner either at Maura's or here at Laura's. These were the nights the family would get together, rain or shine, in sickness or in health.

Laura was older than Maura by three years, but Laura's age didn't show on her the way it did on her sister. For Maura not only smoked, but also drank heavily, and that, Laura knew, was one of the things that got you in the end, made you soft in too many places. Besides, Laura used Noxema and other skin cleansers; Maura didn't believe in beauty products.

There was a time, especially as teenagers, when the sisters looked so much alike that people thought they were twins. Except that sadness had dragged down Maura's smile; even her laughter was sad, often short-lived and forced. Maura's features were dogged by carelessness—the roots of her black hair showed a line of grey, and lipstick never looked quite right on her lips, too often smudged on her front teeth.

Not that she, Laura, paid too much attention to the way she looked, but she did always try to dress her best, anticipating Zacarías's return. There were times when she wore stockings every day no matter how hot.

Why Maura drank, Laura didn't know but could only guess. Maura drank so much that by the middle of the afternoon she was often unbearable—mumbling, antagonistic, insulting, unsteady, and downright obnoxious. Perhaps Maura drank to forget what the family had gone through since they left Cuba. She drank to cope, to deny herself that life could at times be wonderful and full of surprises.

Or perhaps merely because she was an alcoholic and didn't want to admit it.

Laura planned to ask Maura to call her daughter Celia when she came home from teaching and invite her to dinner. Celia kept Maura's drinking in check.

Laura's only niece lived with her artist boyfriend, her "roommate," as Maura called the young man. Rafael's and Celia's "situation" (their living together) kept Maura edgy, insecure about her daughter's future. Maura felt there was no commitment there, nothing to keep either one from walking out of the relationship.

Both sisters had talked about this until the late hours of the night, when Maura stayed over because she'd had too much to drink to be able to drive home. They talked about how love and romance and what was or wasn't proper today for a young lady had changed since they themselves had been teenagers, especially since the children had grown up in the States. Maura, though, didn't buy it—she had had loose friends in Havana back in the fifties.

"I don't understand it," Maura had repeated. "If they love each other like they say they do, why not make a commitment? Take on the responsibility?"

"That's exactly what they don't want," Laura told her. "They don't want the pressures of marriage."

"'The pressures of marriage,' What pressures? Please, *mi hermana!*"

"What would you prefer?" Laura asked. "That they get married, have the marriage last a year or less, and then get

divorced. Come on, look around you. Our own friends are getting divorced. After so many years."

"Okay, so maybe marriage isn't worth—"

"Oh, it is. I like to think my marriage is."

"But living together—"

"Stop being a Puritan," Laura said. "Don't look at it from
a religious point of view. Or a what-are-the-neighbors-going-
to-think?"

"I don't want to think about it, period."

Maura had stopped looking at her daughter's relationship. She had confessed, "But if I look at it, from any stand-
point, as you say, it breaks my heart."

"Stop being melodramatic."

"How can I not? Celia is my baby, Laura. She's all I
have."

When Maura sounded melodramatic or sentimental, it
was always a good sign that she'd had too many Scotch and
waters.

"You," Maura reminded Laura quite often. "You have
three daughters, one married, another on the way. And give
Cristina some—"

"Cristina's confused. She hasn't the patience for boy-
friends right now. She doesn't know what she wants."

"She's young."

Cristina, Laura's youngest daughter, was driving to
Texas with her friends to participate in a photo-journalism
contest. If Laura told her sister, Maura would worry about
Cristina's safety on the road. From flat tires, busted fan belts,
and running out of gas in the middle of nowhere to hitch-hik-
ers and criminals loose on the road. After all, Laura knew,
her sister worried too much. She always thought of the worse.

If there was one thing Laura had taught all her children,
it was how to take care of themselves.

She would call Maura and ask her to come over, but with
one condition. Laura didn't want to hear her bitch and complain about her daughter's living arrangement, which at this

time was the only thing she talked about. Look at Samuel, Laura thought about her son. Sammy *should* have lived together with Gisell, should have given himself time to find out about Gisell's problems. That way, no surprises when you lived together.

The phone rang then. Thinking that it might be her sister (sometimes she felt there was a telepathic connection between them), she reached over and answered the phone. It was the operator on the line, long distance from Brazil.

"Will you accept the charges?" the operator asked.

"Yes," she said, excited that it was a call from Zacarías.

"Laura?" She didn't recognize the voice over the static and clicking of the line.

"*Bueno?*" she asked.

"Juan Carlos, Laura," he said.

"Oh, Juan Carlos," she said. "How are you?"

Silence. One of those awkward silences people reserve for bad news.

"I don't know how to say this."

The premonition that something was wrong struck her. "What happened, Juan Carlos?"

"Zacarías has had a heart attack."

She leaned back against the kitchen wall and knocked a hand-painted porcelain plate off the wall. The plate hit the floor and shattered.

Her breath left her. *I should have gone with him*, she thought.

"I am here," Juan Carlos said, "at the hospital. They have him in intensive care."

"Where?"

He told her to what part of São Paulo Zacarías had been taken.

"Let me speak to him."

"No, I'm not in the room with him," he said. "I'm in the lobby. They won't let me in to see him."

"I don't believe it," she said, stepping over pieces of the broken plate.

"He has the best care, Laura. I am making sure of it."

"Is he all right?" she asked, and her voice trembled. "I mean, how *is* he?"

"Laura, don't worry. The doctors have it all under control."

The doctors have it all under control, she repeated. "Tell Zacarías I will be there as soon as I can get on a flight. Tell him that for me, Juan Carlos," she said. "Please stay with him."

Juan Carlos promised her he would, and his voice faded out. Back on the line, coming through crisp and clear, he told her again not to worry, that he'd see to everything.

"I am leaving right now." She neither said goodbye nor hung up. A bone-deep chill got the best of her. She wasted little time in dialing information to get the American Airlines number at the airport.

The next available flight out of Miami to Brazil departed at 3 p.m.

"Direct flight?" Laura asked.

"No, it makes a stop in Rio."

"Book me on it."

Laura quickly noted all the vital flight information, then thanked the agent and hung up. She needed a ride to the airport. Maura would take her. She dialed her sister's number, but the line was busy.

Don't waste any more time! she told herself. The last minutes of the morning ticked away.

As fast as she could, while she tried to get through to her sister, Laura jotted down a list of things she had to do before the flight. She needed to find her passport and put it in her purse.

What might Zacarías need over there? Pajamas. A bathrobe. A pair of slippers. She blamed herself for all this; she should have warned him not to go so far from her.

Thoughts came too fast as her list grew. She kept redialing,
waiting for her sister's line to clear.

৯০৬

3

Why Some Women Drink

Maura drank alone. Her stashed Scotch whisky tasted better that way. Alone. No husband. No daughter. Only silence for company. Drinking helped her smooth out the rough edges, took the bite out of her bitterness. She sat at the round table, facing the front door, the bottle of the amber colored elixir by her side, within reach, and drank to make herself stop thinking.

There she sat with her gray-streaked black hair draped over her face, covering her bloodshot eyes.

Thoughts of the old days came to her. Days when she had hopes and aspirations. But those days were *poof*! Gone.

Drinking made the bad thoughts go away; thoughts of death and suicide. How many times had she not contemplated the absolute end? The various ways of leaving this life, this situation... this world—this harsh and intolerable reality.

She drank to bring back her dead parents. Her father and mother, whom she'd give anything to have alive. But in this life there were no such miracles. Besides, why would she want her parents back in this world? They suffered enough the first time around. Why have them do it again?

Once, she drank so much that she wanted to go to a palm reader. She wanted to see María, a woman better known as *La Machetona*. The Machete woman? She didn't know what *machetona* meant, but that was what the woman called herself. María, the clairvoyant. Maura thought that María could help her, through a séance, bring her parents back.

The afternoon she decided to go visit María, she remembered, she was alone then as she was now, and she had already drunk a bottle and had broken the seal on another. She got in the car and drove it straight into the garage door. The loud splintering and crushing of the wood didn't startle her; didn't alarm the neighbors. She put the car, a four-door olive-green Buick, in reverse and drove out of the driveway at such a speed that the wheels screeched and skidded against the loose gravel of the driveway, sending gravel flying from under the tires.

She didn't get far. The car picked up so much speed within a distance of two blocks that when she hit the banyan tree on Ferdinand Street, it crashed and broke through the hard tendrils of the tree then stopped when it hit the trunk. She was unconscious by the time the paramedics arrived, pulled her out of the car, put her on a stretcher, and drove her away to Coral Gables Hospital. Her left leg was shattered and twisted beyond repair. Even now, after so many surgeries, her leg was an ugly sight. The orthopedic surgeon on duty in the emergency ward did his best, but his best left her with an obvious limp.

Yes, she drank to forget that and so many other things. She went on drinking binges when she was alone. Alone in this house she no longer looked after, she no longer enjoyed, that which no longer gave her any pleasure.

She gazed around the room and decided that the house was hopeless. Casa Maura, as her house was called by the family, was a simple, two-story white house which, with patience and a little money, could be fixed up and made to look right out of *House Beautiful*.

It stood in the heart of Coral Gables, the most beautiful city in South Florida. An original city, not one of these prefab enclose-me-in, security-ridden neighborhoods. This was a city that cared more about dirt and trees than about cement and traffic lights. No billboards here. To get to this city you had to know the names of the streets. Unlike the rest of Miami, there was no number system here, which is so much better.

The names on the streets helped keep out the riffraff of every-day traffic.

Like Celia, who now lived with her boyfriend in an apart-ment on Mendoza Street on the other side of Ponce de Leon, said once, "Not even Domino's Pizza delivers here."

At first Maura didn't understand what her daughter meant, but then she remember the time gimmick: Domino's guarantee of speedy delivery or the customer got a discount.

There was no better system for privacy than this in Coral Gables.

Her mind was freewheeling again. Fast-forwarding. Rewinding.

It didn't matter to her in what direction her mind sped. She sipped her Scotch on the rocks and smoked one menthol cigarette after another.

The wide French windows shaded by the round blue awnings allowed a view of the garden and Ferdinand Street. The house, built in 1923, stood covered with English ivy and bougainvillea. The vines grew and stretched as far as the garage, which sixty-seven years ago had been the carriage house. Still with its intricately carved wooden doors, it was now used as Norberto's office. But because it is illegal to have anything but a garage in Coral Gables, it still looked like one from the outside. Norberto used the converted place whenever he was in town, which was seldom.

It was in the attic of the garage where Maura hid her stash of liquor. So far, neither her husband nor her daughter had found it.

Was she an alcoholic? Laura had asked her to ask herself. Was she? She was and she wasn't. There was no black or white, only gray. Sometimes she indulged more; sometimes less. Did she drink for pleasure or because of an insatiable need? From habit? Because of pain? And why couldn't she talk to her family about her pain? Maura thought she drank because it was the only way to keep herself company. No one should be blamed for her drinking, not even herself. *She* *drank, she drank, her breath stank...*she made the rhyme in English, a language she understood better than she spoke. She drank because the children (Celia, her daughter, as well as her nephew and her nieces) had grown up. She had lost purpose, direction, aim, meaning, whatever she wanted to call it.

What happened to the family? What happened to those wonderful years when they lived in Lomas Verdes, Mexico City. The whole family, her parents included. Her parents were alive and happy then. So was she. Her nephew, nieces, and daughter had grown up. So what if they still visited? It wasn't the same anymore. So what if they still saw each other on Thursdays during dinner, whenever they were in town. Thank God Celia graduated and decided to move to Miami. But now, now she'd moved out of her room and into her own apartment.

Maura tried to think of the details of how Celia met that young man, but...God only knew.

The children had grown up... This was the house where Celia grew up. It was the same house where Maura spent her days cleaning, cooking, drinking (drinking mostly), talking on the phone to her friends. The house, she imagined when she'd had too much to drink, was haunted. Haunted by the old ghosts.

But it was a wonderful, joyful time—she drank only on special occasions, to socialize. To aid her in conversation. The dinners on Thursdays got re-established back then. She and Laura produced the most elaborate dinners. She cooked; Laura made things look pretty. That was her job.

Zacarías Senior, "Papi" Torres, was alive and as charming as ever. He wore colorful bow ties that made him look like Kentucky Fried Chicken's Colonel Sanders....

She drank because she damned well knew she couldn't bring back those days. Everybody was dead now, or waiting to die. Not the children, they still had many years left. She hated to admit that life, her life at least, was a big joke. If there was a God (when she drank she found it hard to believe in one). He must be playing a rather cruel, sick joke on humanity.

She stood up to get more ice. The telephone rang, but she decided not to answer it. She was through listening to her friends gossip. It rang for the longest time, then it stopped. The ringing lingered in her mind. After the drink was ready, she decided to disconnect the phone.

With drink in hand, she walked to the stairway where all the pictures of the family, in dusty frames and smudged glass, hung. Over-exposure to light had turned the older pictures into faded streaks of sepia. Light or the years? She settled for the years—those damned bastards.

On this wall was the history, the progressions (and digressions?) of the Almendros-Torres clan. There were more women in this family than men. She and Laura were married to twins. Not identical, of course. Physically Zacarías and Norberto couldn't be more different from each other.

Maura leaned for support against the handrails to the stairs—her arms folded over her belly, drink in hand—and stared at the pictures. Sometimes she laughed because she remembered something funny, heard the voices echo in her head.

Here were wedding pictures. Birthday parties of the five children. School and graduation portraits. Most of the wall was devoted to the children's evolution. The most recent pictures were the wedding 8-by-10 glossies of Samuel's marriage to Gisell and of Sofía's to Ariel, that Argentine scoundrel.

Looking at the pictures helped her pass the time.

Another trick.

ৡৡ

It was Thursday afternoon and Maura was in the kitchen, again replenishing her drink, when she heard the front door unlock, and her sister Laura, dressed in black pants, a lavender blouse, and a leather jacket in hand, walked in.

Crying, Laura was crying, and her eye make-up ran.

Maura left the drink by the telephone, which was still disconnected, and walked into the living room.

"Zacarías had a heart attack," Laura said.

Maura felt a little numb and unsteady as she went over and embraced Laura. Why would this happen to you, *mi hermana?* she thought as she held on to Laura.

"I've got to go," Laura said. "This afternoon's flight to Brazil. I went crazy calling you. Is the phone off the hook?"

Maura asked about Zacarías's condition.

Laura told her what she knew, what Juan Carlos had told her over the phone.

A quick sobering was now taking place. Maura said she wanted to accompany Laura on the trip.

"No," Laura said, "I need you to stay here. Look after these things for me." Her sister put a folded piece of paper in Maura's shaking hands.

A list of things to do while Laura was away. Maura offered to drive Laura to the airport.

"You've been drinking," Laura told her in a calm tone of voice, not accusing.

She could drive.

"No," Laura added, "I will leave the car in the overnight parking."

Maura neither felt ashamed nor guilty. Her brother-in-law's condition worried her.

Laura said she had to leave for the airport. "I need you to call everybody. The children. Round them up and tell them what has happened. The numbers are on the list. I need you to stay sober, Maura." She then gathered her jacket and purse. She was ready to leave.

Maura realized how much her hands were sweating. Shaking. So she put the list down on the coffee table. She must take care of this list as if it were a treasure map.

"Also, keep the line clear," said Laura. "I will call you as soon as I see him."

Maura kissed and embraced Laura goodbye, then returned to the kitchen, hung up the phone, and took a big gulp of her diluting whisky. She listened to Laura's car pull out of the driveway.

She drank the rest of her whisky, got more ice into her glass, and poured herself a stiff one, stronger and meaner than the last. She needed this one drink, she said to herself, more than any other, to pull herself together. To get through. This one drink before she turned her concentration and energy on her sister's list.

Finally, this was why she drank: because bad news plagued her life. Bad news had a way of always finding her.

കംഗ

4
All-American High

SEX, DRUGS & ROCK AND ROLL! read the crooked letters marked with what looked like lipstick on the dented and
bent lid of the tampon dispenser. Celia stood next to it looking
at her irritated red eyes in the broken mirror of the ladies'
room in the teachers' lounge. Her whole face was puffed up
and yellowish in complexion. After she finished splashing
water into her eyes—which during any other time when her
allergies left her alone were clear and light ocher—she couldn't
believe it, she thought, these damned allergies were driving
her crazy. How much longer could she endure the itch? The
inflamed eyelids and the constant watering and burning?

All day the other teachers had been giving her strange
looks, staying out of her way, not saying hello, as if her allergies were contagious. But she knew better. They were all fed
up with the educational system; the masses couldn't be edu-
cated, not by them anyway, and they all knew it but didn't do
anything about it. So everybody was always miserable and in
a foul mood, constantly risking public outrages.

She sneezed, and her whole head felt like it was going to
explode since her ears were plugged up and her nose was
watery in one nostril, congested in the other. What was it
anyway? Dust, pollen, cat hair, ash particles from the burning
Everglades—all of these fucking things mixed in the air?

Celia pushed her straight, shoulder-length black hair
over her ears and decided against more make-up, for she
looked sick and nothing would help. Rafael, her lover, told her
all the time she looked like Frida Kahlo because of her thick

eyebrows and high cheek bones, and today Celia felt so shitty and miserable that she tried to believe him.

She was sick. For days now she'd been dripping—that's what she called it, dripping—and snot wasn't the only thing she dripped. The cramps had started, and they came strong and hard, the punctual shits. Her stomach muscles went into spasms, tightened and knotted to let her know her period was here.

One more sneeze and she felt her congested chest tighten. In her purse she found the box of Actifed, the over-the-counter antihistamine she bought at Publix every time she went in for cigarettes. Actifed was her salvation; the Roto-Rooter for her clogged pipes. She snapped two little tablets, more like M & Ms, out of their plastic bubbles, and pushed them back into her throat. She needed to stop smoking and get back on the BC pills since her cramps were less severe when she was on the pill. And besides that, she didn't want to get pregnant.

Only the hot water faucet worked, so she grabbed her coffee mug, rinsed it and poured a little hot water in it, waited for it to cool, then drank and swallowed her antihistamine pills. It would be at least twenty minutes of more itching and suffering before the pills took effect. One thing though, which she didn't mind—in fact she like it—was the strange rush caused by mixing the pills and the caffeine.

In the mirror, she straightened out the collar of her Paisley shirt, smoothed the wrinkles of her skirt, wiped her irritated nose with her fingers, and rinsed her fingers in the hot water.

She decided to go back to her classroom a little early and rest her feet, get some peace and quiet. On her way out of the bathroom, on the back of the bathroom door, she read the sign: *HOW DO YOU SPELL RELIEF?* Below the scribbled letters someone had drawn a large penis with a disproportionate helmeted head and hairy balls. She pulled the door and walked out.

Celia had been teaching at this high school in Homestead, Florida, for a semester, and she was already contemplating quitting. Why was she doing it anyway? Surely for the money—even if the pay wasn't really that high, it was still the highest salary she'd ever been paid—and also for all the time off.

Six months ago she had graduated from the University of Florida with a bachelor's in American Literature. Her parents told her to take some time off, that she didn't need to start work right away; she had wanted to plunge in—now she was way over her head, overburdened with work and bullshit red tape, tense, stressed out, fidgety, anxious, on the verge of blowing a fuse, as her father would say.

A couple of days ago she got into an argument over the phone with one of her student's mother. The boy's mother didn't want her son to read *Lord of The Flies* because the family preacher had told her that this book was the devil's work. Celia told her to read the book, inform herself, and stop being ignorant. The woman hung up on her and called the principal to complain.

On the periphery of the avocado-colored carpet of the lounge, Celia was greeted by Gordon, the union stewart. Next to him, she was small, *petit* was the word, for Celia was an inch short of being five feet tall, whereas Gordon was a huge tower at six feet.

The moment he saw her, he flung his arms up in the air and said, "Pay up, Celia!" Gordon rolled his eyes up at the ceiling. "Pay up now!"

He was talking about the union dues, which, since she was contemplating quitting teaching come June, she didn't intend to pay.

"I'll pay as you soon as I—"

"That's what you tell me *all* the time," Gordon said, then insisted, "Matter of fact, you've been telling me that since the beginning of the semester. Matter of fact, since you started to work here. You know everybody's got to pay dues. Dues are dues."

Vicky, a fellow teacher, walked into the lounge and said, "Celia, you've got a call in the office."

Celia answered the call in the mail room; it was her mother, Maura, who apologized for calling, but that there had been an accident.

When Celia heard the word *accident* from her mother, she thought, what had she done to herself this time? Celia built up enough courage to ask her what had happened.

"Bad news," Maura said.

"What happened to you?"

"Not me, your uncle. He's had a heart attack."

"Is he alive?"

"We won't know until your aunt gets down there," Maura said.

The bell went off, which meant lunch break was over, and Celia had to be in the classroom soon—her classroom was all the way at the end of the courtyard, by the drivers' education trailer.

"I'll come by after work," Celia told her mother.

"Okay," she said, "but I have everything under control."

"I'm sure you do, mother."

"But maybe you can help me call everybody."

"I'll be there by three-thirty."

"Don't speed."

"I've got to go," Celia told her. Her mother clicked the line without saying goodbye.

Celia walked out of the mail room and the main office and, with every step closer to her classroom, thought about her uncle having a heart attack in a foreign country.

Her antihistamines were taking effect, working their magic nicely. Breathing again, she stepped into the classroom as the tardy bell rang. The clamor of the bell echoed in the hallways and crept under the doorway and into the classroom. "Out of time," she said out loud, "Shit!" The word came out of her effortlessly. Her students laughed. Still having difficulty breathing, she didn't know if she would make it through the afternoon.

໔ৎ৯

5

Leaving

Sofía knew about her, the other woman. She also knew that Ariel knew she knew. How could she not know—there was little he was willing to hide or disguise, for the sake of her dignity. The evidence became obvious right away; she found it all over the place. There were the phone calls, and when she answered, the other person hung up. She knew about *her* a few months before he suspected she had found out. Sofía remembered the lipstick (not her color obviously) on his shirt collars, the blondish hair sticking like lint to the lapels of his blazers. Once, Sofía went as far as looking for clues on his underwear, but he had been careful, he wasn't stupid. She found no stains or pubic hair on the front of his bikini briefs. After all, she was certain he was cheating on her, and knowing unleashed a strange hatred within her, from a deep well she didn't know existed. Now it was too late—she didn't want to hear made-up stories or excuses.

She moved through the house in a whirlwind of energy, rummaging through the closets, drawers, cabinets, desks, making a pile of her stuff, packing only essentials into an old suitcase. She intended to leave not a trace of herself. The maids left her alone, but she often felt them looking on in awe. Yes, the maids stayed out of her way as if her anger were contagious and they would all commit horrible acts of vengeance and violence against their own *macho* men. Sofía made little piles all over the place, then told the maids that all her stuff was theirs, that they should remove everything from sight before Ariel got home. "Throw out what you don't want," she told them, "but take everything out of here. Burn it, I don't care."

The maids could not believe their eyes; they thought Sofía had gone insane.

All Sofía wanted to do now was get away from the *pendejo*. She realized what a shit Ariel was. She wanted to return to Miami. Buenos Aires had been nothing but a waste of time. She was through with Argentina, with its people and their make-believe European ways, with him. Ariel was history; he could not be anything else to her now.

Their marriage, which lasted two years, was over. They had dated longer than that after they met in Miami while he was attending a computer convention. They saw each other for the first time in the hotel bar. After that day, he returned to Buenos Aires and started to call her every day. It didn't take him long to find an excuse to return to Miami.

How could she have been so easily fooled? She should have known that behind the suave, European look there'd be deceit and betrayal.

From the top of the nightstand in the bedroom, she picked up a picture of her and Ariel—she sitting on his favorite Arabian horse, a smile on her face and her short, cropped hair slicked back over her ears, and he sitting behind her. She threw it on the pile of clothes and assorted memorabilia.

His almost aquamarine eyes had done strange things to her, had put a charm on her when she looked into them. Then he invited her to visit Argentina, and she accepted.

No more. She refused to think about those memories. Instead of focusing on how things were, she should keep in mind all the little shitty things Ariel had done to her in the past two years. Like his affairs. How many women had there been?

She didn't blame the other woman, for it was his fault and his only, not the other woman's, and as far as she was concerned, she, Sofía, had been a loving wife, up until she

found out about his Argentine flame. See, she followed Ariel
to a restaurant on a night he had called from work to say that
he'd not be home for dinner. Of course not, not dinner. But
she followed him to a hotel, and saw him in the lobby with the
other woman.

After that, Sofía returned to the house and thought of
murder: ground glass in his dinner, a clean shot between the
eyes, or, even better, castration while he slept, she fantasized.
For the next few days she didn't confront him. Then she
decided not to confront him. Now she was leaving for good.

She blamed him for being careless and heartless and, in
the end, stupid. He didn't have to do it behind her back; he
could have told her, "I'm having an affair. I don't love you
anymore." The effect would have been the same except that
she would have been spared the humiliation. She might have
felt respect for him. People do fall out of love, sometimes a lot
sooner than they think.

Sofía found herself in the living room, their "love nest" as
Ariel called their apartment. She was done gathering all her
things, and Margarita and Trini, the *muchachas*, were
already picking through the dresses and things that they
were to keep or give away.

She asked Emilio, the family chauffeur, to get the car
ready and take her to the airport. She was leaving later in the
afternoon for Miami. She was going to disappear, he'd see,
and return to her parents' house where she'd have all the
time in the world to think things out, look for a way to begin
again. Maybe she'd enroll in a university in the States and
finish her degree in marine biology.

She stood there by the living room window and looked out
at the busy, crowded streets. The children played soccer,
kicked the ball against the sides of parked cars. Yes, she
would go away, leaving not a trace of herself, and Ariel would
return home and find her gone.

Down on the street, Emilio leaned against the side of the
Mercedes and waited for either Margarita or Trini to come

down and tell him *La Señora* was ready. He was a strong man in his late fifties, around her father's age, and he was kind and appreciative. For the last two years, he had been her handyman. She never got a "no" from him. She'd give him the car, she decided—after all it was in her name as it had been a birthday gift from Ariel, when he thought a gift of this magnitude would make her happy. Emilio would think that she had gone crazy. Let him, she thought. In the end it would be the same. She didn't exist as far as this place was concerned.

Margarita called, "*Señora Sofía, todo está listo.*" Everything was ready.

"Margarita," Sofía said. These were the first words she had spoken since this morning. "Tell me something."

"What, *Señora?*"

She turned away from the children playing in the street and faced Margarita, a young woman, one year older than Sofía.

"Are you feeling well, *Señora?*" Margarita said. "I can make you some chamomile or linden flower tea?"

"No, I feel fine, Margarita. Thank you."

Silence. It was awkward for both of them. Sofía having no more things to tell her to do, and Margarita standing there empty handed, on the verge of being jobless.

"When Ariel returns," Sofía finally spoke.

"*Sí, Señora,*" Margarita answered.

"Tell him I've disappeared."

The word in Spanish was *desaparecida*. The word in Argentina had a special meaning everybody understood. It had to do with all the people who had been killed or put in concentration camps during periods of political repression.

"Tell him that. Nothing more, nothing less. You understand?"

Margarita nodded, understanding, with none of her pleasant smiles now, and seemingly on the verge of tears. Sofía told her the reason why she was leaving. Now Margarita looked sadder and more depressed.

"Men are no good," Margarita told her with assurance.

They fell silent, as if pondering this truth, then Margarita said, "So everything's ready."

"Everything, *Señora*."

Sofía told her to ring Emilio downstairs and have him carry the bags to her car.

Margarita rushed to call Emilio.

Once again Sofía turned to the window and saw the children being chased away from the street by the baker and his broom. If she was to miss anything about Argentina, it would be the beautiful children.

The phone rang. She let it ring for a while, deciding not to answer it.

Margarita and Emilio entered the living room. The phone was still ringing. Margarita hurried to answer, but Sofía stopped her. "Let it ring, don't answer it."

The phone rang several more times, then stopped.

Silence engulfed them in the living room.

Emilio carried the bags, and Sofía and Margarita followed him to the car. Margarita was staying behind to look after the apartment until Ariel returned.

Downstairs by the car, Sofía hugged Margarita as they said goodbye. "Where is Trini?" she asked.

"You know how she is," Margarita said. "She's very…"

"Tell her I said goodbye."

Emilio opened the car door for her. She climbed in and put on her sunglasses. She was leaving this place for good, she thought. As Emilio drove away, Sofía waved at a crying Margarita. Emilio looked up at the rearview mirror. She caught his eyes. He gave her a sad glance. No need to speak, she thought, for he knew where she wanted to go now. He would take her there and, like old friends, they'd say their goodbyes.

She had already disappeared.

&∞&

6

Golden Baby

Beatriz was back in Mexico City, the place of her birth twenty-four years ago. This was her city, even smoggy and crowded beyond tolerance, beyond belief. A black fine soot hung thick in the air, stuck to the skin, which would take a lot of scrubbing with a sponge in the bath to wash off. The smell of chipotle chili and freshly baked tortillas mixed in the air as the breeze swept it along the streets and building entrances.

It was her first full day back in town, back into the hustle and bustle, the movement of things. Wheeling and dealing. Streets filled with vendors and Indian women who sat on the sidewalks. They spent their days weaving to earn enough money to feed their children. Where were these women's men? she thought as she and Lorenzo, her fiance, walked by. So many people. The color and commotion overwhelmed her.

The place, for better or worse, lacked direction, organization, but that was the way she always remembered it. Beatriz liked it this way.

It was like a giant rainbowed tail of a kite, colorful and forever in motion, swirling into pockets of desire and passion. People gathered on the streets, waited in doorways and by street lamps. Old women looked out their apartment windows or stood dressed in thin, worn dresses on balconies. All of them had that hungry look on their dark faces. Sullen eyes.

Beatriz was out, out on the city. Walking hand in hand with her soon-to-be husband. Give it time. In less than a year. Patience was a virtue, her mother told her once. If she had patience, everything would turn out right for her. In no time she would be called Señora Beatriz Torres de Carrillo. She loved the way that sounded.

The twangy sounds of Mariachi music faded in and out from the deep penumbra of small restaurants. The latest Emmanuel song, "*La Chica de Humo*," blared from a stereo somewhere.

They were walking the vastness of El Zócalo. The church and buildings around El Templo Mayor were sinking slowly. They gave her a sense of warped perspective. Lorenzo held her hand. His were calloused, rough. She liked the feel of them. He recently graduated as an officer from the Mexican Naval Academy on the Cuauhtemoc, a sailing school ship— one of the most beautiful sailboats she'd ever seen.

He squeezed her hand. She was giddy, overjoyed. He called her his golden baby. It was a name Lorenzo had heard Zacarías call her. Golden Baby. Sometimes, to get her mad, he called her his Cubanita or Cubita. She hated that name, for the only thing Cuban about her were her parents. Miss Beatriz Torres, she thought, *was* Mexican—it was in her blood, the sights and sounds of this city.

At a street corner they stopped to listen to an *organillero*, an organ grinder, who turned the handle on his instrument with zest. The sound the organ made carried her back to when she was a little girl living in the city, to those Sundays after mass when the whole family visited these same sights.

"What happened to the monkeys?" she asked, remembering that every organ grinder had a monkey.

"They've all died," Lorenzo told her.

The organ grinder looked at them, turned the sound in their direction. Lorenzo pulled a one-thousand peso coin out of his pocket and threw it into the open organ case.

"*Gracias, Señor*," the organ grinder said, and bowed to Beatriz.

"Why can't they get new monkeys?" she asked Lorenzo.

"Monkeys don't reproduce in Mexico. They like their privacy, you know," he said. "Besides, when these guys get real hungry, the monkeys—"

"*No seas*," she said, stopping him from elaborating.

Lorenzo laughed and hugged her.

"I think you should take me out dancing tonight," she said.

"I thought we were having dinner at your parents."

"After."

"All right. We'll go dancing."

"I will dance like a monkey for you," he said, "Especially since you miss the little critters that much."

Now she laughed.

"Or we..."

There was a pause. He released his grip around her.

"What?"

"We can do a little fooling around of our own."

"*Fooling around*," she said.

"Yes, isn't that what the gringos call it?"

"That's what they call it," she added. "But there won't be any 'fooling around' until after the you know what."

"Cruel, cruel."

"That's me."

Last Christmas Lorenzo and his family flew to Miami so that Lorenzo could ask Zacarías for Beatriz's hand in marriage. It was the formal thing to do, and her parents turned the gathering into a big celebration. Everybody, herself included, got drunk. That was the night her father made the big speech about his losing his precious golden baby. After that night, Lorenzo started calling her *his* golden baby. "The gold is in her eyes. Her skin," her father said.

"I guess," Lorenzo said, pulling her along as they walked down the crowded cobblestone plaza. "A good thing is well worth the wait."

They kissed.

"Should we start heading back?" he asked.

"What time is dinner?"

"Seven."

"Let's go then."

They started to head back toward the main streets where they could catch a taxi. Once again she lost herself in this city carved in bricks. The high archways housed the pigeon and sparrow nests. As they walked back, pigeons set aflutter formed beautiful waves.

ତ~ଚ

They took a taxi back to Lomas Verdes, where Lorenzo's parents lived. The house had belonged to Beatriz's aunt and uncle during the sixties. It was here that she and her brother and sisters and cousin Celia spent their early childhood. When her uncle Norberto got a job in Miami, they sold the house to the Carrillos. That's how she, who stayed for several more years, met Lorenzo.

Lomas Verdes hadn't changed. Things didn't change much in Mexico except for the increasing number of people and the smog in the air.

It was an immense city. They got stuck in the dense *periférico* traffic. The ride back took more than an hour. As the taxi pulled up in front of the house in Lomas Verdes, Aurora, Lorenzo's mother, was there to greet them.

"Beatriz," she said, "your aunt called this afternoon. Shortly after you two left."

"Why?" From the saddened expression on Aurora's face, Beatriz perceived that something bad had happened.

"Your father has had a heart attack."

"Is he alive?" the words came out of her mouth automatically.

"Maura didn't say," Aurora told her. "She didn't know either."

"You must go back," Lorenzo said.

"Maybe before you do anything, you should call Maura," Aurora said. "Find out more."

Good idea, Beatriz thought. She would call her aunt and get the details before she made any hasty decisions. She went into the house, picked up the living room phone, and dialed Maura's number. But nothing happened. She dialed the operator, who told her all the lines were busy. She must wait.

Fifteen minutes later, her call went through. Maura's voice was muffled by the static of the distance. She told Beatriz all the information she knew about her father's heart attack, which wasn't much. Laura was on the way.

"I don't know where to go."

"Stay put," Maura said. "I promise I will call you back as soon as I hear from your mother."

"How about my brother and sisters, have you called them?"

Maura couldn't get through to Sofía. No one answered in Argentina. She called Samuel, but he was at work. She spoke to Gisell. And Cristina, she didn't know where Cristina was.

"Keep trying to reach them," Beatriz said.

"I am."

Beatriz told her aunt that if need be she would meet her mother in Brazil. Again, Maura said Beatriz should wait for her call.

"Do you think he is all right, *Tía*?"

"I don't know," answered Maura.

When she hung up with her aunt, Lorenzo came to Beatriz's side. He had been listening to the conversation.

"I'll go with you," Lorenzo said.

"I'm not going anywhere until Maura calls me back," she said. "Besides, you can't leave the country. Don't you have to be back on duty?"

"Not until Tuesday. We have plenty of time," he said.

"I don't know how much time I have."

Aurora said, "You are only going to get in the way, *hijo*."

"But I don't want her to go alone," he said to his mother.

She hated to have to leave Mexico so soon, but she'd have to once Maura called her back. She'd be back, she told herself.

Now she thought of her father and wondered whether he was
alive or dead.

౭❀ఇ

7

Eagles Have a Real Thing for Freshly Road-Killed Armadillos

Cristina was on the road to Texas. She was almost out of Florida, nearing Pensacola. This was exciting, she thought. Grace and her boyfriend Nubi were with her, driving straight on through Northern Florida. Luscious panhandle scenery, green and hilly. Nubi drove the Maxima. He kept practicing his heavy Texas drawl, which, since he was from Saudi Arabia, sounded really funny. "Howdi Parrrrrner!" he said. All three of them laughed. "How 'bout a col beeeer?"

The sun roof was open and the breeze was hitting Cristina in the back seat. Her hair flew and fluttered into the sides of her face, eyes, and into her mouth.

"Ah, speed is a wonderful thing, no?" Nubi said.

He was going eighty-five. She wondered if the Maxima could take it, would take it.

He said, "That's the nice thin' bout cars. Give 'em gas, they go."

Grace leaned back on her seat. She was all smiles, been so since they left Miami. She'd been Cristina's friend since junior high, the seventh grade, the year her parents moved to Miami from Mexico. Grace met Nubi at Fiorucci's where they all worked. Cristina worked there part time. Now she devoted all her time to her photography, which was the reason they were going to Texas. Cristina had entered a photo-shoot contest, and even though she didn't have to be there, she thought she should, considering this was her first contest.

"Slow down, Nubi," Grace said. "I don't think the highway patrolman's going to appreciate your speed."

"My speed'll smoke 'im," he said. "Whoever he is."

"Their cars are faster than this one."

"C'mon, this is our flying carpet."

"It's more like an area rug," said Cristina.

Nubi looked up at the rearview mirror. He smiled at her.

"Don't worry, Cristina, the H.P. will not catch me."

"Do you know what H.P. means in Spanish?"

Grace knew. She'd heard it before, but she waited for Cristina to say it before she smiled.

"*Hijo de puta!*" Cristina said.

Nubi tried to repeat it, but it came out something like *High de put.*

Grace, slowly, spelled it: "*H-i-j-o d-e p-u-t-a.*"

"*Hijoss de putaa.*"

"He's getting it."

"What does it mean?" Nubi asked.

"Son of a bitch."

Nubi laughed, and his straight white teeth flashed. He was perfect for Grace, Cristina thought, with his model-type looks.

They approached the next rest area. Nubi said, "O.K. Who needs to go twinkle?"

"Tinkle," Grace told him. Then, "I do. I gotta go."

"I can wait," said Cristina.

Nubi turned on the turn signal, looked at the side and rearview mirrors, and exited the highway. Eventually he had to slow down. The rest area was full.

They stopped. Grace jumped out and ran to the bathroom.

It was while they waited for Grace that Cristina spotted the great bird in the distance. It was tearing the flesh from a animal killed on the road. The bird—an eagle?—pulled long strips of flesh from what looked like an armadillo with its beak and claws the color of blood.

"Look at that!" Nubi said.

She reached for her Cannon in her bag. While she changed to a telephoto lens, she prayed that the eagle wouldn't fly away. One look in that direction assured her it wouldn't. Crows started to land around the carcass, and every time they hopped close to the flesh, the eagle batted its wings at them. The crows had no choice but to stay back, peck at the empty earth. It was a great bird, an eagle, with white and grey plumage on its head and breast.

"It's tearing it to—" Nubi began to say, then in a low voice, "to pieces."

Finished with the lenses, Cristina opened the car door and stepped out. She moved carefully, slowly.

"Where are you going?" Nubi called after her.

"Stay put," Cristina told him and waved at him to stay back in the car.

She approached the eagle with the stealth of a cat, aimed, focused, and shot. The whirring of the automatic loader wasn't loud enough to scare the bird. She captured the eagle, bright-eyed, looking straight at the camera, a piece of pinkish red flesh hanging from its sharp looking beak.

This was wonderful, Cristina thought.

"Cristina!" Grace shouted from behind her. "What's going on?"

The bird shot skyward, lifting a whirlwind of dust and dry leaves. Cristina took half a dozen pictures of it in flight, then stopped to watch it fly away.

"You fucked it up, Grace," Cristina told her friend, turning in her direction.

"What? What?"

"My shoot," Cristina responded.

"A bird's a bird," her friend said.

"Don't be stupid." She now moved in for close-up shots of the carcass. "That's not any bird. It was an eagle."

Burs stuck to her socks. She would pull them off later.

"Well, we'll never get to New Orleans at this rate," Grace said.

"You were the one who made us stop," Cristina shot back. "Anyway, what's your hurry?"

Grace shrugged.

She was trigger-happy now, shooting the carcass of the dead armadillo. Flies swarmed about the open wounds. Cristina managed to capture the rictus of death. Part of the animal, its hind legs and back, were crushed against the asphalt. Tire marks on the drying fur. A truck must have hit it.

Grace came to see the dead animal, then moved away.

"Just a couple more shots," Cristina said.

"I'm going to throw up."

"Use the bathroom," Nubi told her.

Grace disappeared into the bathroom.

Cristina looked up at him and smiled.

"What?" he asked.

A wonderful idea dawned on her.

"I'm going to enter these pictures into the contest."

"Instead of the others?"

"Exactly."

"Will you have time to develop and mount them?" Nubi asked.

"We don't have that much time, I know, but I can do it. These are *the* ones."

Today was Thursday, she figured. All they needed to do was drive straight through to Corpus Christi, Texas, where the college was. She told this to Nubi, who said, "I don't know if we'll make it without stopping."

"We'll take turns driving," Cristina suggested.

"Sleep'll get us."

"O.K. We'll rent a motel room." She thought about this. "Hey, that'll give me time to develop these." For this trip, she carried her developing equipment.

Once again Grace returned from the bathroom. She was pale.

"Cristina says she wants to drive on through," Nubi said to her.

"But New Orleans," she said.

"We'll catch it on the way back."

"O.K., let's go," Nubi said.

They all climbed in the car and Nubi drove away from the rest area. In no time, he was back doing eighty-five miles per hour.

"I want you to stop every time you see a dead animal by the side of the road."

"Are you kidding?" Grace asked.

"I'm serious. You too, Grace. Tell me when you see a carcass."

"You are crazy," Grace said.

They got into a long conversation about the new project she had in mind. Cristina told them she'd been inspired. Eagles Have a Real Thing for Freshly Road-Killed Armadillos, she decided to call her new series. Grace thought otherwise, saying it was a gruesome idea. But were there armadillos all along the southern states, all the way to Texas? She asked her friends.

"I'm sure there are," Grace said. "But not all are going to be dead. What do you want, Cristina? For them to stop, get hit by a truck, so you can take their picture?"

"She's right," Nubi added. "Better change it to any animal, whatever we find dead."

Good idea, she thought. That would provide variety. She was excited by the prospect now. So excited, in fact, that she forgot she was supposed to call her mother to inform her of her present whereabouts.

৵৽

8
Talk

Gisell began:

This day, this hour, this instant.

Her days passed fragmented, broken up.

She woke up tired.

Couldn't concentrate on anything.

She was bored.

Restless.

What would she do? she asked herself.

Every morning, damn it, she must face her mortality, the way she looked into the mirror and hated her looks.

Mostly she despised her eyes, for they were nondescript. Sparkless. And oh, her bleached hair.

No smile.

No lips.

She wasn't ugly, she knew that, but she wasn't beautiful either.

She was fed up with the raptures in her thought patterns.

One second she thought of one thing, and blam! something else completely different the next.

Couldn't concentrate.

When this happened, she'd much rather not think at all.

Rid her mind of worthless thoughts and ideas.

All her thoughts and ideas were worthless.

Silence.

Stasis.

...maybe she should commit herself.

But she had already gone through that.

Sane people were the ones in asylums, and she was insane.

Insane, she focused on that word.

The hours passed. Her days. Her moments.

Nothing was accomplished, nothing got done.

Sure, she worked.

Something to pass the time.

She was a secretary for Stead & Barnes, an engineering firm that did contract work for the U.S. Navy.

Samuel, Sammy her husband, an engineer himself, got her the job.

Sammy The Smarty.

She didn't get it on her own. No siree, she got a big push from hubby.

Sammy salami, in-fucking-tense!

She couldn't stand her lack of motivation.

She felt like that gooey green stuff kids played with. What was that called?

She needed to do something.

Act.

Maybe kill herself.

She was an emotional retard.

Something dramatic, yes.

Slash her wrists.

Watch the blood ooze out of her.

What she really needed was cannabis—it worked wonders.

That'd slow her thinking down.

It always did.

Fragmentation.

Happy drugs.

They made her happy, something she hadn't been in a long time.

When she got like this, in these uncertain moods, she knew she never would be happy.

Fuck the silence. Fuck ideas. Fuck her ugliness.

Fuckafuckafuckafuckafuckafuckafuckafucka—

Talk about her mantra.

Or in-fucking...

Fuck her lack of motivation. Fuck!

That's what she needed, another thing she needed. She needed to get fucked by Samuel. Samuel, her fucker. Hubby fucker Samuel.

Sammy The Sneak who buried in her his salami while she pretended to be asleep.

And he suffered from the 2:00 a.m. sneakies.

But the bastard was at work; she was here in the doc's office.

Talking. Talking up a storm of words. Not really, talking—thinking.

Talk, the woman doctor bitch (for playing devil's advocate all the time, doing it so well) told her.

Talk, talk, talk.

Get everything out of the fucking system.

Off her chest.

Her breasts had started to droop.

How could she tell?

Because she kept a measuring tape in the bathroom.

Taped to the wall.

Everyday she pointed her nipples at the tape and charted their position.

It was slow, the droop, but they *were* drooping.

She'd gained weight too.

No, she refused to stop eating.

For Christ's sake, that was all she had left these days.

A prolonged pause.

She was pensive now.

The system was between her legs.

The clock ticked, and she knew she'd have to pay whether she said one thing or a million of them.

She decided to talk and cleanse her body and mind and mouth of all that ailed her.

Fucking impurities.

It wasn't like this was her first or second visit here.

She'd been visiting shrinks (pardon the expression) all her life.

Don't worry about repetition.

Talk. Simply talk.

She was crying.

She began with her days, past fragmented, broken up, like a plate busted into shards in the kitchen sink.

Yo hablo, she said, *tú hablas, él habla*. Everybody talks.

Her in-laws.

She knew they talked about her. Nasty things about her warped personality.

The way she had Samuel on a leash.

By the balls.

Also her sisters-in-law.

They talked about her the most.

Call it paranoia.

They talked about her!

She began to begin. (Wasn't that a Julio Iglesias' song?)

Her days in Maryland. No, more specifically, Washington D.C., outside of which they (she and Samuel) lived. Began dull and dreary.

She made them thus.

By thinking too much about what she was going to do with her days.

Her time.

Stop worrying about the days.

Anyway, living in Maryland was the pits. She was bored. She didn't know anybody outside the circle of people she'd met at work.

Because of work.

And what a circle!

They were all ugly and gruesome like herself.

Why was she constantly putting herself down?

Because she couldn't put herself up, now could she?

It took energy; hers was depleted.

A low ebb.

Anyway, they didn't get along. At all.

Damn Samuel for bringing her up here.

Another thing, another thing:

The fucking winters here. Shit! Harsh, harsher that she'd ever been in.

She was a tropical child, from the island of Cuba. Know where that was? In the Caribbean, of course.

Off course.

Trouble there got her here. Her parents got her out because of their troubles there.

Now Samuel's brought her up here, away from the warmth of Miami.

It was his fault if she was so unhappy.

Listen: the reason why she was here was because this morning she really really contemplated leaving Samuel and Maryland and hitting the road and returning to Miami. Listen, she really really thought about it.

Still did.

So much so that she didn't go to work.

She told Samuel she wasn't feeling well.

This was something she had been thinking about for a long long time.

Plotting.

Samuel believed everything she said.

He believed her words, not her actions. Or was it the other way around?

Samuel also did everything she told him to do.

Anyway, that was when Maura called.

Maura called and disturbed her morning nap, and God knew she didn't get another chance, not so often.

"Zacarías has had a heart attack," Maura told her.

Her father-in-law. A heart attack? she thought. Maybe he was dead.

Alone, she didn't know what to do.

She panicked easily.

Immediately after she hung up with Maura, she dialed the office. Samuel was nowhere to be found. The first two people she spoke to didn't know where her husband was. The third, another secretary like herself, told her Samuel had gone on a day trip to Newport News. Off to the docks. Samuel worked on silencing nuclear submarines. It was hard work, he'd told her, silencing those fuckers under water. If a crew member farted, the sound couldn't be heard.

The secretary asked her whether she wanted to leave a message.

Tell him, she began, but then only thought about it: His father was dead of a heart attack.

Unlike what she suffered from.

Mental attacks.

Except no one's died from it yet.

No, no one in her family had a history of mental disorders, not that she was aware of anyway.

Maybe she would call her mother and ask.

Maura hadn't said dead, had she?

See, she was not concentrating again.

She must get a hold of Samuel.

By mid-afternoon, when she hadn't, she couldn't stand the anxiety, so she called her analyst and made an emergency appointment, which cost double.

And now here she was.

෨෧

Talking.

Was she feeling better?

There were days when she did try to feel better.

She knew how lazy she was.

When would she learn to control her anxiety?

It had to come from within, the control.

Sometimes she felt like she was wasting her time and money coming here.

Was she?

There were no answers for that question, but if she felt that strongly then perhaps she should quit.

Quit?

She'd done it before.

She wanted everything to go right, but how could they when now her father-in-law was...was...was—SAY IT! Dead!

Her time was up.

She had so many things to do.

Call Samuel.

Tell him the news.

Decide whether they would fly or drive.

Yes, Samuel would want to fly down.

Pack.

She felt it again. Pressure and anxiety. She closed her eyes, breathed deeply, regulated the air she consumed.

Her time...

She knew.

Look at it this way, she thought, now she got to go to Miami. Get away from having to work. And the cold.

From people who played silly games like Dungeons & Dragons and called that partying.

From focusing on her marriage.

Her marriage was no piece of cake.

She was, would be shortly, Miami bound.

Except.

Except that aside from her parents, everybody would be happy to see Samuel, but not her and—

Her time was definitely up!

&∞&

9

Bad News

From Rio the plane flew on to São Paulo. As she walked out of the gate, she spotted the man holding up a placard with her name on it: *SEÑORA LAURA TORRES*. She approached the man. He greeted her, then introduced himself as Castello, a friend and co-worker of her husband.

"Juan Carlos sent me to meet you," he said to her in Portoñol, a mixture of Portuguese and Spanish.

Laura understood. She asked Castello what he knew of her husband or his condition.

"Very little," Castello said. All he knew was that her husband was in intensive care. Juan Carlos would know more.

Downstairs in baggage pick-up, Castello grabbed her only suitcase and carried it outside where he hailed a taxi. It was muggy outside, and the air was thick with exhaust and diesel.

She climbed into the taxi, and Castello told the driver where to go. The trip to the hospital seemed to last a long time, but they finally arrived. Castello paid the driver and once again took charge of the suitcase. Laura hurried into the fluorescent light of the emergency ward, through the sliding doors. Castello asked a nurse for direction. "ICU is here," the nurse informed them. "Through those doors." The nurse pointed in the general direction. Castello said he'd wait in the main lobby.

Down the corridor in the distance, through the glass, she recognized Juan Carlos sitting on a lounge chair. When he saw her, he hurried to her. His eyes were bloodshot and tired, or had he been crying?

"Oh, Laura," he said and reached for her. He embraced her.

And suddenly she knew. He didn't have to tell her anything. Zacarías didn't make it. In his arms, her legs grew weak and gave out on her. He helped her over to a chair.

"A massive coronary," he said, still holding on to her.

Her mind went blank. She felt lost and confused. Dizzy.

Juan Carlos continued, "The doctors tried their best."

Suddenly, she stood, became frantic. "I want to see him now," she said.

Juan Carlos took her by the hand and led her. He introduced her to the head nurse of ICU, who took them down a hallway, and they turned left into another room.

She repeated to herself that it couldn't be, her husband could not be dead.

Once she entered ICU, the sound of machines, the soft voices of the nurses and doctors bombarded her. She heard nothing and yet everything, including the tiniest of hisses, ticks, white noise. She couldn't believe her husband had lost his life here among so much technology. What good was it? Expertise. And nothing saved him!

Finally, they reached the part of ICU where they kept the deceased before sending their corpses off to the morgue. The examination table on which Zacarías's body rested came up to her waist. A sheet covered her husband, all of him, from head to feet.

"I'll be outside," the nurse said.

Laura pulled back the sheet and exposed her husband's face and chest. His eyes were closed. Also, the skin had lost all color. When she looked at his chest, she felt her own heart skip a beat. They had opened his chest and left a wide incision. His shaved chest was darkened with spots that looked like dried blood.

She turned to her husband's face again, stared at it for a long time as if expecting him to open his eyes any minute now.

Any minute now, she thought. *You will open your eyes and see me, your wife. I am your wife who loves you. Open your eyes. Look at me.*

But Zacarías's face was forever peaceful.

Again, she grew weak, but Juan Carlos was there to prop her up and keep her steady.

She needed strength.

"He didn't suffer," Juan Carlos said.

How did he know? she wondered.

She looked at Juan Carlos.

"I stayed with him all along."

A doctor approached them and told Laura how sorry he was. He assured her that all was tried and done to save her husband. "We have an excellent staff here," the young doctor said.

An excellent staff couldn't save him, she thought.

"His heart was not strong," the doctor told Laura, "but his will to live was. It was very strong."

She broke down. Juan Carlos took her out of the room and back to the corridor. He stood her next to the open window. The nurse brought Laura cold water. She was sweating.

She drank the water, but it didn't make her feel any better.

Once she sat down, she closed her eyes and thought why Zacarías. Why him? God, all the things left unsaid. She couldn't bear it. Her lungs filled with grief.

Juan Carlos stood by, silent, arms crossed, not knowing how he could offer comfort.

"I want to take him back with me," she said. "As soon as possible."

"You've had a long trip," Juan Carlos said.

From far away in the other rooms came the white noises. The beeping and ticking and sighs of machines, and sick people dying. She sat on the chair and pondered how she'd get Zacarías back to Miami; she didn't know where to start, but Zacarías belonged there. Close to the family.

She must also have strength to be there for the children.

Zacarías was dead, may God provide for him a place in Heaven and let his soul rest in peace!

৵৹৵

Tercera

Evening

10

Flying Projectiles

Instead of driving straight to her apartment after work, Celia stopped by her mother's house to find out more about her uncle. Her mother didn't live too far from Celia. Coral Gables was divided into three sections: the residential area (where her mother lived), the downtown and Miracle Mile shopping district, and apartment row, where Celia lived with her boyfriend. She would call Rafael from her mother's and tell him she'd be on her way in a while.

Maura's car was in the driveway. A couple of cats sat on its hood. Celia pulled up behind her mother's car and killed the engine. The noise startled the cats. One of them jumped off, the other, a lazy tabby cat, stretched, yawned and began to clean itself.

She liked cats, had two Siamese, one named Wasabi and the other Sato. Both were gifts from Rafael.

Getting out of the car, she realized she was leaving the key in the ignition. So what, she thought, this was Coral Gables—nobody stole cars here. Once she climbed up the three steps that lead to the porch where the white and yellow rattan chairs stood surrounded by plants, she knocked on the door. She noticed that the mailman had left the mail by the door. She picked it up. Hadn't her mother gone out at all today?

Nobody answered.

She tried knocking with the brass door knocker. Louder. If her mother was upstairs or taking a shower, she would not be able to hear the door.

Celia used to have a key, but she lost it.

One last knock, and when nothing happened, she decided to try the kitchen door. Her mother often left it open. Celia walked around the garage between her mother's house and the neighbor's. The neighbor's children were playing in the swimming pool, being supervised by the baby-sitter who looked suspiciously at Celia as she came around the house.
The children said hello as she walked by. Celia returned the greeting with a smile, a weak one at that, the kind she reserved for her students when they were up to no good.

Couth, her dog, barked at her when she untied the gate of the fence that enclosed the backyard. He wagged his tail, his pink tongue dangling stupidly from the corner of his mouth.

"Hi, Couthy," she said to the dog.

He began to run the length of the yard, perhaps thinking he would get to play. She would ask her mother if Couth had been fed.

Celia tried the kitchen door and it was unlocked. She stepped in and called her mother. Reaching into the fridge for something cold to drink, she called again. Maybe her mother stepped out with one of her friends. A few lived up the street. Maybe they picked her up.

She found a quart of orange juice and poured herself a glassful. Her allergies had gone away for now. She was feeling much better thanks to the antihistamines she took earlier.

As soon as she walked into the dining room, she found her mother on the living room couch. Her arm dangled from the edge of the sofa, fingers barely touching the wood of the floors. First Celia thought the worst, but then she heard the breathing, and immediately Celia knew what was wrong, her mother had passed out.

Celia approached the sofa. On top of the coffee table was an empty glass. Celia picked it up and sniffed—J&B Scotch whisky. Drank herself out, she realized. Her mother's blue veined feet were dirty, dusty, as if she had been walking barefoot outside.

"Mother!" she called close to her face.

Out cold.

Celia figured something bad must have happened when her mother drank herself to sleep like this. Her uncle must have... she took the glass and an ashtray full of cigarette butts (most of them smoked down to the filter) to the kitchen. She emptied the ashtray in the kitchen trash can.

Suddenly, she felt angry. Gnashing her teeth, she turned around and hurled the empty whisky glass in her hand against the cupboards. The glass shattered, but she was so furious and her mother so gone that neither were startled by the sound.

"You'll see," she said loud enough for her mother to hear.

In a flurry of anger and hatred for what her mother chose to do to herself, Celia searched the whole house and gathered every single bottle of liquor, perfume, rubbing alcohol, cooking wine, sherry, even glasses, and smashed them into the trash can. Pieces of glass flew everywhere. When the trash can was full, she smashed the remaining bottles against the walls. Bottle after bottle, she didn't stop to look at all that glass. The splashes spotted the walls.

Celia did not find what her mother drank or bought, her stash. She knew it had to be here somewhere. From the key holder in the kitchen, she removed the keys to the garage. If the stash wasn't inside the house, it must be in the garage. She'd find it.

Her mother would get the hint that it was time to stop her drinking.

In the garage the musty smells of her father's files and mildewing paper lingered. The humidity was thick. Celia went ahead and looked through the filing cabinets, behind the books and magazine stacks on the shelves. Inside the closets, but failed to turn up her mother's supply.

She was sweating.

Celia wondered whether her mother buried her stash somewhere in the backyard. But, no, then she would have had

to dig it up every time she ran out. She stopped her search to
look outside and around the garage. Nothing.

How about in Couth's house or under it? No, she figured,
because Couth would dig it up, drag it out.

She returned to the inside of the garage. Her father had
seldom used the office when he had the garage converted. She
made up her mind that her mother's liquor had to be here.

It was then that she looked up and saw the trap door
inside the closet. She rolled her father's desk chair to the spot
right below and climbed on top of it. She pushed the trap door
and slid it back and thump! It knocked against something.
She was too short to have a look, so she jumped and pulled
herself up holding onto the frame.

She grabbed the brown paper bags and threw them
through the trap door against the floor. One by one, the bottles shattered, and the sound told her she'd found the stash—
struck gold, struck deep where it hurt her mother's habit.

She climbed down and counted the soaked paper bags.
Seven in total. All whisky from the smell of them.

Whisky no more!

She would leave the mess and let her mother find it.
Maura would get the message.

Celia realized, as she had many other times before, that
nothing could keep her mother from buying more liquor. But
that was all right. Let her buy more, she'd break them, too.
She'd always find her mother's stash. Wherever her mother
hid the bottles, Celia would sniff them out and destroy them.
Seek and destroy. Somebody was bound to win.

Back in the house she pondered whether to put her
mother in bed or leave her on the couch. Her mother was too
heavy for Celia to lift up the stairs.

Let her sleep there on the couch, Celia told herself, and
walked to the table to scribble a note.

She found a list of things to do, written in her aunt's
handwriting. Also on the note were the names of Sofía and

Beatriz and their telephone numbers. Next to Cristina's name were several question marks.

Came by. I am very disappointed. Why do you do it, mother? When are you going to start behaving like an adult? I came by to find out about my uncle, and I find you like this. What's going on? Call me, Celia wrote. She didn't sign her name, but tucked the piece of paper under a vase on the table.

She dialed her apartment phone number. The phone rang three times and the recording machine came on: "Rafael and Celia are not home right now," the message began. "After the beep, leave us the best of what's on your mind."

"Rafa, are you there? Answer the phone," Celia said, and waited.

Rafael was not home.

"O.K.," she told the machine. "I'm on my way home."

She hung up. He was usually home in the afternoon. Celia checked on her mother one last time. Maura was still breathing hard. Still out.

Outside, Couth barked, so Celia found two cans of Alpo in the pantry, opened them, and took them outside. Slowly, so that he wouldn't run out, she opened the gate and dumped the food on his dish. He ate it down fast.

Back inside the house, she changed her mind about the note, returned to the table and took the piece of paper, crumbled it, and left. She knew, note or no note, that her mother would get the message.

ॐ◌ॐ

11

Roadside Casualties

The fragility of life confounded Cristina. Here were all these innocent creatures, out for food during the night and they got run over. Headlights blinded them and they stopped in the middle of the road and smash! Most cities had their road maintenance crews clean up the carcasses, but out on the fringes, between towns, between cities, between the vast distances that united this country, the animals decomposed. Sometimes, if they were smaller, like mice and rabbits, they were eaten and only their blood or some other excreted fluids remained on the road as testimony.

Feathers and pieces of fur were also telling clues as to how an animal died. When a dog got thrown out of a moving car or pickup and run over, all that lingered after a while was the broken fur, the signs of the struggle to survive. With limbs broken, internally bleeding, a dog might make it to the shoulder, then it succumbed there to a slow and painful death. By noon of the next day, it would be bloated and the maggots would soon appear on the open wounds.

Cristina was capturing the essence of all this with her camera, in her photographs. Consumed by the impetus of this new idea, her trip to Texas with her friends seemed a lot shorter. So far Grace had spotted a dog, a raccoon, a snake, one rabbit and many mice, including one with tire marks on its flattened body. Mice, by the roadside, seemed to be more prolific, thus it was only natural that more got run over. People threw junk food out of their car windows: potato chips, cheese nachos, popcorn, half-eaten sandwiches or spoiled hot dogs.

They had seen three dead toads, all flattened. Their lives squashed out of them by a tire. By the force of a single deadly blow. It was all found here on the road.

What took up most of their time at each stop was changing lenses, arranging the perfect shot. The right angle could be as telling and meaningful as the content of the photograph.

For example, earlier that afternoon, Nubi (they all did simultaneously, but Nubi wanted the credit) spotted a dog. On closer inspection, the dog turned out to be a Labrador retriever. (While she moved and readied for the shots, Grace and Nubi stayed back in the car and Cristina caught them making out a couple of times.) She took a roll of pictures on that one dog—of its mouth, bloody and toothless, the missing eye, the cracked skull, and the remaining half of the body. The hind legs and tail were gone. Fragmented shots which she would later mount in one display, one frame, and all the pictures would then recreate the whole dog, bring him back so to speak.

In Mississippi, she remembered to stop and call her mother, but still no one was answering at her house. Evening was upon them.

"She must have gone out," Grace said to Cristina.

"Maybe," Cristina said.

Nubi came out of the rest-area bathroom with his fly half unzipped. Cristina noticed it before Grace. Grace pointed it out to him.

"Ah," he said. "Unfinished business."

He laughed.

Back in the car, they drove on while Cristina removed one of the lenses, cleaned it, and prepared the camera for night shoots, all of them on the lookout for more roadside casualties.

સ્જેન્ડ

12
Their Arrangement

Theirs was a one bedroom, upstairs apartment on Mendoza Street, a few blocks away from Miracle Mile in Coral Gables. Celia parked on the street, and as she got out of the car, she looked up to see if the windows in the bedroom were open or the bedroom was lit. Rafael didn't like air conditioning, and when he painted, he liked to have a lot of light. Light brought out color, so he'd told her several times.

The adrenaline rush faded, but she still thought about her mother. Her drinking had become a problem. Maybe if she, Celia, started attending A.L.A.N.O.N., a branch of Alcoholics Anonymous for friends and family of alcoholics, her mother might get the hint and start trying to do something about her problems.

Celia began to climb the dark stairway of the poorly maintained building—the property held by a bank after the owners declared Chapter 11 bankruptcy. Jane, the mother, the single parent, the ex-wife, the divorcee, the hyperactive workaholic, I-get-no-respect/I-get-no-rest next-door neighbor, stepped out of her apartment door.

The minute she saw Celia, Jane began to talk. Jane's biggest problem was her seventeen-year old daughter who, Rafael claimed, liked to ditch school and call her boyfriend and get him to come over.

"She's a rabbit," Rafael told Celia one afternoon. "Jane's daughter. It seems like her hormones have kicked in—" The rest of that conversation almost became an argument. Was he jealous? Perhaps he wanted to be in the boyfriend's position. Maybe...

Jane's eyes, jade in color, were always surrounded by red. Celia knew more about this woman's personal life than about anyone else's. Celia figured that perhaps the reason why she'd become Jane's confidant was because they were across-the-way neighbors. It was easy for Jane to open her door and knock on hers. What Jane needed was stability, Celia thought. Rafael always said that what Jane needed was a man. Rafael had been accused of being a macho artist by *The Miami Herald*, a woman art critic called him that after his last show.

They became acquainted a year ago when she and Rafael moved into this building because they fell in love with the parquet floors. She liked wood floors; Rafael went crazy over the five windows in their bedroom—all that light coming in. They found the apartment the first afternoon they had been out apartment hunting and rented it.

"The owner," Jane was saying, "came by today and asked for the rent money."

Celia didn't know how to stop Jane once she started with a monologue. She was too polite, Celia realized. Why didn't she have that same kind of patience with her mother?

Jane continued: "The conniving bitch has the guts to tell me that they have not received the rent check. And she wanted me to write her another. Can you believe it? So I say to her, 'I wrote you guys a check on the first. I always send it out on the first. You know that.' She says, 'Well, we don't have it and we need that money.' So I tell her to wait while I call my bank to find out whether the check has been cashed. Suddenly, the owner's face changes. She steps back and tells me that it's all right, she'll check on it. Shoot, 'she'll check on it.' Right. I wasn't born yesterday, lady. So after she leaves, I call the bank anyway and inquire about my check. The teller says to me that the check was paid. It made me furious. Can you believe the nerve that woman has?"

Celia stood there thinking she believed anything, anything was possible.

"I immediately called those people and gave them a piece of my mind."

"Good for you," Celia said.

The downstairs door opened and someone came up. Celia looked to see if it was Rafael, but it was Jane's daughter with a hand over her eye.

The minute Jane saw her daughter, she asked her what happened to the eye.

"Leave me alone," the daughter said, and tried to enter the apartment. But Jane blocked the way. Short, but gutsy, Celia thought. The daughter, Meredith, must have inherited her size from her father.

Jane repeated, "What happened to the eye?"

"Got into a fight."

"At school?"

"No."

"Did you go to school?"

"No."

"Why the hell not, young lady?"

"None of your business."

Right then and there Jane belted her kid one across the face. The daughter didn't say anything. Didn't respond to pain either, and Jane whacked her hard.

Meredith pushed Jane out of the way and entered the apartment.

Jane stood there and smiled awkwardly, totally embarrassed by the scene.

From the kitchen behind the partly closed door came the sounds of things flying across the room and breaking.

"I better put a stop to it," Jane said to Celia. "Thanks for listening."

Celia smiled, thinking that they had both had an awful, tiring, and trying day.

She was glad to be able to get away. That kid did need to be set straight.

Celia put the key in and opened the door. She flipped on the light in the kitchen and quickly noticed that everything was clean. Picked up. No dirty dishes in the sink, coffee and butter-stained silverware on the counter, or half-filled glasses with either coke or milk.

She set her purse on top of the table, kicked off her shoes. Her feet felt numb.

"Rafael!" she called out, but no one answered.

The white noise of the aquarium filters reached her in the kitchen. Water flowed and bubbled on the surface as it was being filtered clean.

Rafael kept fish. He was filling up the small apartment with aquariums. Had five already, two were fifty-five gallon monsters which he kept in the bedroom. Enough water in them to flood the bedroom if they broke. She imagined water ankle-deep and the fish swimming about... "Helps me think," Rafael had said.

She checked the messages on the machine. The only one was the one she left him a while ago, when she had called from her mother's

The machine whirred and clicked... "Rafa, are you there?..."

She pressed the ERASE button and the message stopped. More whirring and clicking. She left the machine on and stepped away from the kitchen. She went to the bathroom.

What a day she'd been having. Had. It was over now. In a way she was glad Rafael was not home, for she was tired of talking. She needed a hot bath, that was what she needed to unwind and bring her body back from the ache and numbness. In the bedroom she removed her clothes and stared at the fluorescent-lit aquariums. The fish darted back and forth, which made her wonder if they were hungry. She probably startled them.

Another look revealed something dreadful. A small fish was doing loops in the water, being followed by a gang of other bigger fish. The little one was being nibbled to death.

Its fins gone, it did that awkward swirl and loop swim to get away. She fought the impulse to stick her arms in the water and save the little fish, but Rafael had told her not to tamper with the water, that any small trace of skin lotion or perfume would get in the water and kill all the fish.

Outside a door opened and slammed shut.

Then she heard Jane's voice: "IF YOU GO AWAY, DON'T COME BACK. YOU HEAR ME?"

Naked, Celia walked from the bedroom to the bathroom, turned on the tub's faucet, stopped the drain, and waited for hot water to fill the bathtub. She sat on the toilet and removed her tampon. Flushing the toilet, she stood and opened the medicine cabinet, reached for the toothpaste, dabbed a little of it on her toothbrush, and brushed her teeth. The motion made her stare at herself. Her eyes were still veiny. Her hair had grown, she thought, since she last cut it. At least it wasn't falling out from the stress.

The tub was half-full, so she got in. The water was hot, too hot, but she knew it would do her muscles and bones good. Slowly, she sat and leaned back. She sighed. Soon enough the steam enveloped her. She breathed in the moisture. A sort of unwinding took place, and she closed her eyes and relaxed.

Next thing she knew the water was spilling over the edge of the tub. She must have fallen asleep. She reached over and turned off the faucet, removed the stopper from the drain, and immediately the water was sucked down.

The spillage had just happened; there wasn't too much water on the bathroom floor. She threw a couple of towels on the floor.

Footsteps came from behind the door.

"Rafa?" she asked.

"I'm home," his voice said.

"Step in here a sec."

The bathroom door opened and Rafael stood in the doorway. He was dressed in a paint-splattered T-shirt and jeans. His black Reeboks, too, were paint-splattered.

"I didn't want to disturb your bath."

"Where were you?"

"At the gallery," he said. "Setting up the show."

"You have to set up yourself?"

"If you want it done right, you better."

"Opus, right? The one on Ponce de Leon?"

"The same."

She looked at him and smiled. She liked the way he looked in his work clothes. The paint on his skin.

He asked about her day.

It was the wrong question since the last thing she wanted to do was recapitulate, but she was polite. Today, except for the occurrence at her mother's, she'd been the embodiment of politeness. "It's been a bitch of a day."

She told him about her uncle having a heart attack and her mother passing out, and work.

"Shit," he said. "If I make some money, you better quit."

He was trying to be sweet, she understood.

"I can't quit until June."

"You might be..."

"Crazy by then, yes."

He looked at her and smiled.

"I'll make it," she said, and stood. She did it because he would look at her. "Come summer," she continued, "I won't have to think about work."

"We can go to the beach," he said, and removed his T-shirt. His arms, chest and stomach were white. All that indoor work, she thought. He needed all the sun he could get; so did she for that matter. They needed to spend some time at the beach. That was the first thing they needed to do come summer.

She dried herself.

Opening the medicine cabinet, he drew a Gillete disposable razor, shaving cream, and proceeded to shave. He sideglanced at her. "By the way," he said. "I'm sorry about last night."

Their little skirmish last night, she thought, and she had almost forgotten. That's why he cleaned up the place...an argument about their financial situation. She mentioned the fact that once school was over, she was not going to have enough money to pay for all his bills. This upset him. He slammed his fist against the table. They were having dinner, and when he hit the table the plates and silverware jumped, rattled against the wood.

"Things'll work out," she told him now.

She thought it was sexy how he shaved, so much foam over his jaw and cheek bones.

"Should let a beard grow," she said.

"Hey, yeah, a beard," he said. Then, "I'll get some olive-green uniforms and some cigars and go to my gallery opening dressed like you know who."

She smiled.

"Imagine all the paintings I will sell in this town looking like Fidel," he said.

She was ready to step out and leave him the bathroom.

"Don't go," he said. "Stay and talk."

She sat on the toilet again and watched him undress.

At one time in his life, she figured, he must have been athletic because his legs were strong. When he lived in Spain and played a lot of soccer. But now, he had a pot belly from too much good food and beer. Her eyes drifted to that dark area of jet-black pubic hair and his penis, the way it dangled like some kind of root—a deflated balloon sticking to the body.

Rafael stepped in the tub and began to take a shower. Except for his art work, he did everything fast. In no time he had shampooed his hair and worked up a lather on his body.

"So what's up with your uncle?" he asked.

"I don't know. Nobody's heard anything."

"What part of the world is he in now?"

"Brazil."

"I couldn't do that, you know."

"What?" She looked at his ass through the transparent flamingo shower curtain.

"Fly in and out of places," he said, and rinsed himself. "I couldn't concentrate on anything, and work least of all."

"He's a workaholic."

"I'm a workaholic, of sorts."

"Yes, but you don't have to travel."

Rafael finished with his shower. In and out. She told him about the fish, the victim in that one bedroom aquarium.

"Nibbled to death," he said. "That's how most of those Neon Tetras have gone. Weak little shits."

They both left the bathroom. She with a towel wrapped around her chest; he naked. Tall, white, and chubby, that was her Rafael. He had a coffee-colored birthmark, the shape of a butterfly's wing, on his back.

Immediately, Rafael turned his attention to his fish. Those hungry horny bastards. The ones called Mollies, the black ones, only knew how to do one thing: fuck. The male stayed behind the female, chased after her, and while he chased, he inserted his prod into her, between her anal fins. Sneaky fuckers. Rafael kept one male for every five females, most of which were swollen with broods. They looked like droplets of tar in the clear water.

"What are we doing about dinner?" she asked.

He said, without looking at her, "What do you have in mind?"

"Something other than dinner," she added.

He looked at her and said, "Then why did you ask about dinner?"

"I'm hungry," she said, "but I'd much rather fool around."

"I see."

"Let's do like them."

"Are you sure?"

"They seem to like it."

Rafael jumped on the mattress and got behind her. He sniffed at her ass. He was imitating the male Mollie.

"Your prod isn't ready," she said and laughed.

"Give me a sec," he said. Then, "It's tough, you know, so many fish in the tank to keep happy."

She pushed him away and said, "There are, are there?"

"Only one Mollie Queen though."

"Well, buster, you let me know when there is more than one of us in the water with you. I don't—"

"You're the only one, my dear. Only one."

"So what do we do about your limp..."

"This," he said and grabbed his penis. "It's almost ready." She watched him stroke it.

"Maybe I can help it along."

She knew she had many worries, but she also knew how to forget about them while they made love, intense and sweet, enveloped in the blue light of the aquariums.

కాళ్ళ

13

Back in the U.S.A.

Being a naturalized U.S. citizen and having nothing to declare, Sofía cleared customs at Miami International without any delays. She decided to rent a car. She waited to pick up her one bag. Then she went to the rent-a-car counter, settled on Avis. She was about to sign for the car when she realized that she couldn't use her credit card, not if she didn't want Ariel to trace her. She also didn't have enough cash. She didn't want to call home; she wanted to surprise her mother, so Sofía opted for the next best thing under such restricting circumstances: a taxi.

Outside the terminal, bag in hand and in the heat and the choking smell of exhaust, she hailed a taxi. The driver, a young black man wearing a baseball cap backward, came around and helped her with the bag. After she climbed in the back, he got in and they drove away from the terminal.

"Where to, Miss?" he asked in a strange accent. Then she remembered all the Haitians in Miami. They had come by the boatloads after she moved to Argentina. She remembered reading about them in the papers.

"Kendall," she said, and gave the young man her mother's address.

The driver looked up at the rearview mirror and said, "That's a little far."

"You don't drive out there?"

"*Oui, mademoiselle*," he said. Then, "Of course. I take you where you want to go."

Why did he ask then? "Let's go."

"Where you come from?" he inquired.

Sofía noticed that he hadn't turned on the meter. She waited until they had driven out to the exit loop beyond all the terminals, then she asked what was wrong with the meter.

"Nothing," he answered. "We have flat rates to Kendall."

"How much?"

"Twenty-five."

She looked at his eyes looking at her on the rearview mirror.

"Company set price, I didn't," he said.

They entered the perimeter and went around the airport, past the landing strips, which were brightly lit like Christmas trees with rows of green, blue, and red lights.

She was already in and on her way; there was nothing she could do about the price now. Sofía wasn't familiar with the way things worked with taxis and taxi drivers.

"Have long flight?" the driver asked.

"Yes, long flight."

"Where from?"

"Buenos Aires."

"Oh, yes. That's long way."

A clanking noise came from the taxi's engine as it climbed the ramp to enter the expressway.

Already, she could tell that the driver was taking the long way home. He should be on the 826 south, not the 836 which lead east. She told the driver the best way to get there.

"I get you there, *mademoiselle*. Trust me. Remember, flat rate?"

She'd never trust another man in her life, she said to herself. Maybe her brother and father, her uncle too, for they were her family.

And her family would soon be drilling her with questions about what had happened between her and Ariel. She might as well make a tape with all the answers:

What happened?

Ariel cheated on her.

How did she know?

She just knew. Call it instinct. The tricks of being a housewife. Men didn't realize women could detect those things. The slight scents, the lipstick...but she caught him red-handed, how was that for proof?

So she left him.

Here she was, in Miami.

What was she going to do?

She didn't know the answer to that question.

Why was she hiding? Did he hit her, abuse her?

No, she just didn't want to deal with him. Didn't want to hear his name, his voice. The bastard would get the hint eventually.

"You mind a little music?" asked the taxi driver.

She returned from her thoughts. "Excuse me?"

"Music," he said. "You like?"

"Sure," she answered. "Music is fine."

The music came on and it was fine because she could hardly hear it in the back. The driver switched from 836 to I-95 south—he was definitely taking her the long way.

Too many lights on the way down U.S. 1, on which I-95 south dumped all its traffic. They caught all the red lights. The stop-go, stop-go, made her carsick.

She realized how much her hands were sweating. By the time she got to her parents' house, she'd be a mess. Though she wanted to surprise her mother, she certainly didn't want to give her the wrong impression.

Her mother would welcome her home. Laura was never too crazy about Sofía marrying Ariel. To her Ariel was always a bit unbalanced. It was that look in his eyes when you looked at them. He always tried to avoid eye-to-eye contact. He would only do so, Sofía knew, in business deals.

Feeling a little faint, she tried to roll down the window, but the handle was missing.

"Use this," the driver said, and handed her a pair of pliers.

The tool was heavy, slippery. She put the pliers to the little knob and turned it. She barely managed to crack the window. A little air would do.

She handed the driver the pliers.

On Kendall Drive the driver kept going straight, missing the turn on 83rd Street.

She pointed out his error.

The driver apologized and made an illegal turn. "Nothing to it," he said.

"Now go to the next corner and make a left. The place is called Kendall Point."

He told her about this being his first week on the job, and that he was sorry not to know all the streets and avenues. "I learn quick," he added.

The taxi driver pulled into the right driveway. Only one car parked in front of the garage, Beatriz's, and the house was dark. Sofía wondered if her mother was asleep. She turned to the driver and asked him the time.

"Five-to-eleven," he said.

Her mother might have turned in early.

She knew Beatriz was in Mexico, but Cristina might be home. Or did Cristina go out on Thursday nights?

The driver took the suitcase out of the trunk and set it down by the front door.

"Wait a minute," she told him. "I'm checking to see if I have the keys."

She used to have a set. Then she remembered she gave the key ring to Emilio. She gave him all her keys.

"I left the keys back home," she told the taxi driver.

"Why don't you knock?"

She pressed the doorbell.

She waited.

In the meantime, she handed the driver a twenty and a ten.

"Keep the change." That was the last of her money.

"*Merci.*"

No one answered the door. She rang again. Nothing. She walked out to Cristina's bedroom window and tapped on it with her fingernails. Still nothing. No sign of movement came from within.

"Nobody home," the driver said.

It was impossible, unless they went out to dinner, but they would have been back by now.

"Please wait one more minute," she said.

"Okay."

Sofía walked around the house to the back screen door of the screened pool area. She knocked on her mother's bedroom sliding door.

No answer. Everything inside the house remained dark.

She returned to the front.

"Nobody home," he said.

She told him to leave, that she would wait.

Suddenly, she thought of going to her aunt's house.

"Wait," she said.

The driver stopped on the other side of the cab and put his hands on the hood.

What if they all went out together?

She should call her aunt from a public phone.

Leaving the suitcase behind the crocuses, she got back in the cab and asked the driver to take her to the nearest public phone.

"I sure will learn Kendall now," the driver said, and smiled up at the rearview mirror.

At the corner of Kendall Drive and 57th, the driver spotted a Dairy Farm Store. The neon cow spun on an axis on the sign out front.

The phone was by the side of the building.

Sofía climbed out of the cab, told the driver to wait, picked up the phone and dialed. The phone rang and rang. No answer. All right, she gave up. They had all gone out. She decided to return to her house and wait for her mother to show up.

On the driveway of the house, she thanked the driver and then watched him leave.

If they didn't show up, she'd be stranded for good. But why wouldn't her mother come? Maybe they went to dinner and to the movies. Her parents would be there soon, she figured, as she sat with her back against the suitcase and waited.

దావ

14

Long Distance Call

Beatriz dialed her aunt's number, having not heard from her since earlier that afternoon. It was after eleven o'clock in Mexico City. After dinner, most of Lorenzo's family retired to bed. Only Lorenzo and Aurora stayed up with her.

Nobody answered at Maura's.

Something must have gone wrong, she thought, her father...no, she refused to think of anything negative.

Each time she called, she had to go through the operator. Three times already she'd gotten the same one. By now they recognized each other's voices.

"An emergency," the operator told her.

"My father's had a heart attack."

"Oh, that's too bad. *Lo siento, señorita*."

Beatriz thanked the operator for showing concern. Maybe now the woman would give it a real hard try.

ॐ∞ॐ

A while later, Beatriz dialed her cousin's number. Celia might know what was going on. The call went through, not too much clicking or static noise on the line. Usually the voice on the line sounded scratchy, as if the person on the other end was in need of throat lozenges. The worse she'd ever heard was the time Lorenzo called and his voice sounded computer- ized, like a robot's in a Sci-Fi film.

Rafael answered.

"Hi, Rafa," she told him. "This is Beatriz."

"Hey, *messican*, how are you doing?"

"Worried. Listen, can I speak with Celia?"

"She's out."

"Asleep out?"

"You guessed it," he said, and cleared his throat. "You know how she is about her beauty sleep."

"Have you heard anything about my father?"

"Don't you know?"

"I know about the heart attack."

"That's all I know, too."

She told him she'd been trying to contact Maura for more details.

"I don't know about Maura."

Beatriz could only guess. Something told her that Maura had gotten *pedo*, drunk.

"Has my mother called?"

"I don't think so," he said. Then, "You want me to wake up Celia?"

"No, don't do it," she told him. She was going to have to return to Miami and take charge. Somebody had to be there, especially at a crucial time like this.

Beatriz told Rafael to tell Celia that she would be in Miami by noon, that she was taking the first morning flight out of Mexico City—her mind was made up.

❧

15
Kink

Cristina, Grace and Nubi drove on until late in the evening. Until they couldn't drive anymore without risking vertigo. On the way, Cristina shot more pictures of dead animals. A cat. A crow. A coyote. All dead by the roadside. She must have taken ten rolls.

They stopped at a Quality Inn on the east side of Houston. After getting the room, Nubi and Grace took showers so they wouldn't disturb Cristina's work later, once she set up the darkroom in the bathroom, and went to have dinner. Cristina asked them to bring her back a BLT sandwich and milk.

From the trunk of the Maxima she removed the box with all her developing equipment and materials. Then, in the room's bathroom, as she unpacked and set up, she checked to make sure she didn't forget anything. She wasted little time, since she planned to have all the pictures developed by first light. She would then select the best twenty-five of the bunch and print them on high quality paper.

She divided the bathroom into the dry side, which was the sink area and the top of the toilet, and the wet side, which took up the bathtub and floor. After she set up, she changed into a T-shirt and a pair of shorts and decided to go barefoot.

Shortly after eleven p.m., Grace and Nubi returned to the room. Grace tapped on the bathroom door. "Cristina," she said. "Got the sandwich and juice. They didn't have milk to go."

"I'll be right out," Cristina told her.

She pinned up the last of the negative strips to dry on the line she rigged up along the shower-curtain rod. She came out of the dark of the bathroom. A little quick break to get something in her stomach. The air conditioner was cranked up and it rattled from the corner under the window.

"Thanks for the bite," Cristina said. "How much was it?"

Nubi said, "My treat."

"I want to pay for this one," she said. "You've been treating since we left."

Nubi looked at Grace and smiled. He was standing in front of the TV reading the cable-channel directory.

Grace told Cristina to forget how much the food cost, that it didn't matter. Then she asked, "How are the pictures coming?"

"Set up after you guys left and developed all the rolls. They're up drying."

"You work fast," Nubi added.

"Yeah, Cristina, you might be done early and you can get some shuteye."

"I doubt it," she said. "The hard part is yet to come. Besides, I can sleep in the car on the way."

"No more pictures of dead animals?" Nubi asked.

"No, not unless we find something other than what I've already shot. I think I have what I need."

Grace went over the list of animals. She and Nubi, who had turned on the TV, laughed.

"What you need is an elephant," Grace said.

"No elephants in Texas," Nubi, tickled by the idea, told them.

"I think what I have is good."

Cristina bit into her sandwich. She was famished.

"Did you phone your mom?"

She said that, yes, many times, but nobody answered. Even her aunt's phone rang and nobody answered.

"They went out," her friend said. "Your mom and aunt go out every chance they get."

"I'll try again later," Cristina said. She took one more bite of the last half of the sandwich and wiped her mouth clean. She was full.

Nubi found an action-adventure movie on. He seemed lost in the explosions and rat-tat-tat of machine-gun fire.

"Lower it," Grace said.

He reached over and turned down the volume.

Grace said, "You don't want the manager to come up and knock on our door, do you?"

"That's right," Cristina said. "Remember the dirty look he gave us when we told him all three of us were staying in the same room?"

"This place is empty," Nubi said. "I think we are the only guests staying here."

"Let's not take any chances," Grace said.

"Time for me to get back to the dark room," Cristina said, and drank the last of her orange juice.

"Let me know if you need anything," Grace said to her.

Cristina looked through her bag for a rubber band, found one, combed and tied her hair back into a pony tail, and entered the bathroom.

She turned on the safelight to look over the drying negatives. Magnifying glass in hand, she studied each frame and marked the ones she thought were good enough to develop into proof sheets.

As usual she got lost in the work, and the minutes turned to hours and so on. Time flew by unnoticed. In the dark again, sliding the chosen negatives through the different trays of chemicals, she worked intensely.

From behind the door came the faint sounds of moaning and groaning. From the television? It sounded like Nubi had changed the channel to something for a mature audience. One of those porn movies, Cristina thought.

A knock came at the door. Grace said, "Cristina, I need to use the bathroom."

Cristina let her friend in. Grace closed the door. She was wearing a long T-shirt. She pulled it up, sat on the toilet and peed. Grace whispered, "Listen, give me a signal when you decide to come out? If you have to."

"Okay," Cristina said. She understood.

"I've been dying to try him."

"What kind of a signal?"

"I don't know. Clear your voice."

"You won't hear me. The TV is on."

"I got it. Bang on the wall twice."

"Twice. All right. I'll do that if I have to come out."

Grace tore a piece of toilet paper and wiped herself dry.

"I'll be in here for a long time."

"That's how long we plan to..." Grace giggled.

"Enjoy it," Cristina told Grace as she walked out.

Grace had never been a wild one, Cristina thought, not until high school anyway. Cristina recalled all the dirty things Grace used to say about Mr. Ramos, their twenty-five year old, gorgeous, science teacher. Grace had had the hots for him.

Since then, Grace had gone out with more men than Cristina could keep track of. A lot of them one-night stands. Cristina hated to think that her friend had slept with every single man she'd gone out with. That would make her easy. No, Cristina decided, Grace knew better than that. Besides, with AIDS lurking on the scene, she wouldn't be that stupid.

Also, she must use a condom. No doubt about it.

The first few pictures from the first roll had dried. They were all black and white, and all had turned out magnificently. There was the eagle, eyes peering into the camera, tearing at the armadillo's flesh.

She liked the one with the crows lurking in the background, ready to come and accept the leftovers. But the eagle was greedy. The crows, in all their blackness, looked like members of a chorus in a Greek drama.

Eagles have a real thing for...

❧❧

Later that night or early the following morning, for Cristina had lost track of time and in the dark she couldn't look at the time on her moon-dial watch, Cristina decided to give her mother another try. She knocked on the wall twice, like Grace told her to signal. Slowly, she opened the door and waited for her friend to stop doing it with her boyfriend, if they still were.

The television was still on. The light from the screen flooded the room. On the screen was a computer display with the title of the next film and a countdown to it. *Sweet Cheeks* was the title of the upcoming movie.

Nubi and Grace were not in the room. The bed was empty, sheets strewn over the edge of the mattress. Cristina sat on the side of her bed, picked up the phone and made a collect call to her mother.

The phone, like many times before, rang and rang and nobody answered.

Her mother, she guessed, must be out late, something she only did when her father was out of town.

Then the noise, a chair bumping against the glass sliding door, reached her ears in the room. Cristina approached the curtained window of the balcony and peeked out.

She couldn't believe her eyes.

Nubi was on his knees. Grace sat on a plastic chair and was holding her legs apart. Nubi's head was buried between her thighs.

Cristina felt herself blush as if embarrassed. Neither Nubi nor her friend seemed to be aware of her presence. She felt like she was invading their privacy, but she had become glued to the spot. She looked on, not being able to stop her curiosity.

The moonlight revealed Grace's face with her eyes closed, an expression of deep pleasure fixed on her face. Then she slid off the chair, cradled Nubi between her legs.

How strange, Cristina thought, that she was both repulsed and attracted by the scene. Her friends' love-making didn't trouble Cristina as much as her lingering there, watching. Cristina pulled away from the window and slipped back into the bathroom. She was completely out of breath. Wow! She couldn't believe it.

She found it hard to return her concentration to the work at hand and ahead of her, but she forced herself to do it somehow.

Cristina intended to finish before dawn.

෫෧

16

The Red-Eye Express

Something was wrong.

Gisell could tell. A gut feeling.

Premonition.

At home again, later that afternoon, she called the office and, miraculously it seemed, she found hubby Samuel.

She said, "Your father's had a heart attack."

"Why didn't you call me?"

"What do you think I've been trying to do all fucking day?"

"I was in Newport News."

"NO KIDDING."

Samuel wasn't saying anything. He was smart when he wanted to be. The news hit him hard.

"Sammy?"

"Pack up," he said. "I'll be home right away."

What did he plan to do, walk into a telephone booth and change into a cape and fly down a la Superman?

He added, "I'll call the airport and book the next flight to Miami."

"Stand-by on the next flight? The red-eye non stop?"

"I'll try all the airlines."

How could she tell he didn't have a bit of confidence in her? Dingleberry, dodo bird Samuel. That was her husband. All she needed was a little c-o-n-f-i-d-e-n-c-e.

See what work—too much of it—did to you? Drained you like liquid Drano.

Her new policy was: work little, rest much. Her body. Mind. Mind more than anything else. Exercise her libido. The ego and the id.

She couldn't cope with work.

Not with the pressures, the tensions, the bullshit, the bickering, the little things that gave you an ulcer the size of a melon.

"By the time you get here," she told her husband Samuel, "we'll be all packed and ready to go. What do you want to take?"

"As little as possible," he said.

Travel light, good policy.

When he asked for more details about his father's condition, she told him to call his aunt or his mother.

"See you soon," he said.

"I'm really sorry, honey."

"You sound it," he said.

"What's that supposed to mean?" On the defensive, always. Fuck him.

"Never mind. See you when I get home."

She wished she could cry, but she hadn't been able to in years.

Her tear ducts had dried up a long time ago. Sealed shut.

She felt terrible about Zacarías. Really.

She liked him...really.

They got along as long as they didn't spend more than five minutes in the same room.

Putting aside all their differences, she and her father-in-law could have gotten along, had they tried.

All they needed to do was sit down and talk, get things out in the open, put all their cards on the table, so to speak.

But they hadn't—and that had made all the stinking rotten difference.

When Hubby Sammy hung up, Gisell ran to the medicine cabinet, reached for her pill box, a gift from Mexico, and popped a Xanax, which spelled the same word backwards.

Ah, happy pills.

No pain, no pain.

If she could go through life feeling happy, why not do it?

Start now. The sooner the better.

On the top shelf in the closet, she found the zip-up black traveling bag.

She searched for hers and Sammy's jeans, some T-shirts, comfortable shoes and undies, and threw them into the bag.

She loved it when she packed in a hurry.

Done in no time.

She could rest now.

Back in the living room, she turned on the TV, the idiot box, and vegetated, which was one of her favorite pastimes.

Anything to kill time until Sammy showed up.

That was it; she liked to kill all her time.

What awaited her at the end of so much time killed?

Who gave a fuck.

MTV would do: a new Madonna video. A poppy tune, upbeat, fast, mindless.

This was a good way to be when there was no other way.

Don't think, vegetate!

ॐ

Sammy The Small arrived home.

He was a cyclone of energy, a hurricane come too fast for warnings.

A worried, what-am-I-to-do? expression lingered on his face.

It happened that we die, Gisell thought. Fuck it, we all did, so no reason to get much done. It was the old existential angst. You got fucked in the end no matter what you did.

It was God's sick sense of humor.

Here, Man, this was life, from birth to death, from one hole to another, feel pain, suffer, and—hell...

Time to go.

They took a taxi to the airport.

Did they have enough time for dinner?

She was starving.

"Lost my appetite," he told her.

You had to go on, eating, shitting, fucking.

She was a heartless bitch, she knew.

Samuel told her nobody answered the phone, neither at his mom's or at Casa Maura's.

"The End" by The Doors faintly came to her, and she caught herself humming it under her breath.

"No safety," she said. "No surprise. The end."

"What?"

"Nothing," she said.

Samuel stared at her with that look—she could see it. He was about to blame her.

She felt an argument, a bad scene, rising from behind their silence. A tidal wave. Get out the life vests and the life savers!

He wanted to condemn her.

"I give up," he said.

Give up what? The ship?

Wide-eyed, no smiles, Sick-of-it-all Sam.

"Why give up? What? Give up what?"

"I don't want to argue."

"Neither do I. I'm too happ—" She stopped.

"Say it."

"I took a happy pill, that's what I meant to say."

"Always, the fuckin' pills."

When Hubby Sammy grew excited, his accent got worse. He pronounced his words with strange twists of the tongue.

The airport at this time of the night was full of oddballs, David Lynch movie extras.

All right, if they argued, let them until he'd had enough.

She put up little or no resistance.

After he was done, she said, "I'm staying in Miami." She meant to throw another log into the fire.

"For good."

"To live."

Samuel looked at her and his eyes became glossy marbles. He wanted to cry, but his sense of pride wouldn't let him. He was too macho to weep.

"We do what we have to do," he said, and turned away.

They were sitting at a round table in the coffee shop outside the gate.

Appetite gone, they sat in silence.

They had nothing else left to say to one another.

So anti-climactic, she thought, but so was the nature of their disgust with each other.

"My father might be dead and I don't know it."

She said: "I really am sorry."

End of conversation.

Flight 808, the red-eye express to Miami, Florida, began to board.

It departed on time.

She and Samuel sat apart, a stranger between them.

These were the seats he booked. Sulking Sammy brooded, felt sorry for the way things were turning out.

Gisell pretended to sleep, but couldn't because the stranger next to her was giving her the eyeball. She perceived the wrong vibes from the guy. He smelled bad, too, like yogurt gone bad.

Maybe she was asleep and all this was a dream, maybe so. She no longer cared.

She closed her eyes.

She tried to dream, but nothing happened. Her mind was a perfect blank. Smooth. Boundless.

Flight 808 would land in Miami and her marriage to Samuel The Silent would be over.

Such was her life.

࿇

17

Broken Glass

Light blinded Maura. When she opened her eyes, the splendor pierced her pupils. Quickly, she shut them. What happened? she thought, but her mind was slow finding the answer. She brought her hands up to her mouth and exhaled, blew air into them, and caught a whiff of her breath. What breath. She now knew.

What time was it? What felt like a sledge hammer hit her when she tried to sit up. Getting old, bones and muscles not what they used to be. Her mind was blank. To try to remember anything hurt. She thought that after so many times she had gotten used to hangovers. So many thousands of brain cells dead. Her shoes had disappeared. Finally, after she sat up for a while and her brain got used to the gravity pull, she stood. Slowly, unbalanced, she retraced her steps to the living room and kitchen where she cut her feet on a piece of broken glass. It hurt.

There was broken glass everywhere. How had she managed to do this? The cupboards were empty and the kitchen door was open. Oh, no, she thought, this was not her doing. Then she realized that someone had come by, like her daughter, and done this.

Outside, Couth, the dog, barked at her, jump-started her nerves. Up to now she wasn't feeling much, but the barking...the door to the garage/office was open and...oh, God, there on the floor, shattered, were all her bottles. Her precious stash. It could not be. Why, baby, why must you do this? she said to herself. Of course, she was speaking to her daughter, that bloodhound. Celia could sniff alcohol...should work at the airport, weeding the drunks out of the regular passengers.

Not her bottles. She looked down at the empty soggy paper bags. The torn labels. All the liquor spilled on the floor tiles. She sighed and her lungs filled with fresh air. Her feet bled and she could feel the nasty pangs of pain coming up her legs. Leave it, she thought, get away from here. The sight made her sick.

Maura needed something to stabilize her condition. She felt out of control. Why must it be like this? Her own daughter hated her.

Leaving blood tracks on the floor, she returned to the kitchen, searched for something to drink. Her throat was dry. Her lips cracked. Celia left no spot unturned. She must have looked everywhere, found glass, bottles, cups, anything that reminded her of her poor mother drinking, and shattered them. Ah, her bottles.

Behind the can of Spanish olive oil and spice jars by the stove, she spotted the vinegar. She uncapped it and took a swallow. It was a sharp taste which stung taste buds. She spat into the sink, then rinsed her mouth with water. Get out, and get a drink, she thought. Go to Leo's Liquor. The blood kept oozing from her feet. It surfaced between her toes. She had to do something about the pain.

The blood...she didn't want to draw any attention if she went out. God knew she got enough of that, attention.

Determined to get herself a drink, she walked up the stairs to the bathroom. Would Leo's be open? What time was it? She sat on the edge of the bathtub, opened the hot water faucet and let the water run over her feet. The phone rang. She couldn't answer it right now.

Pieces of glass had cut the bottoms of her feet. When she applied pressure with her thumbs, the blood oozed and streaked. She smelled the alcohol in her breath or was it in her blood? She couldn't see clearly whether she had managed to remove all the minute pieces of broken glass.

What a mess. The bathtub filled to her calves in vermillion-colored water. And she wondered what would stop the flow? Get the glass out first. All the glass. Avoid an infection by dabbing iodine or hydrogen peroxide on the cuts. Her mouth went numb, either from the vinegar or the lack of a drink or both.

While she sat there cleaning her feet, watching how the blood swirled around her legs, it came to her. What happened came to her. Earlier today? Yesterday? What time was it? She needed to know. Her brother-in-law? Laura called and told her Zacarías was dead. No, she came by the house. She left a note. Instructions. A list of things she wanted done.

Again, Maura failed her sister. She had this feeling in the pit of her stomach. Oh, she couldn't bear it any longer. She must have a drink, and have one right away. She stepped out of the tub. Bleeding or not, she had to go.

She went to the bedroom to get a pair of shoes, checked the time: 1:45 a.m. That early? She'd been out since... She hoped Leo's Liquor was still open. If she hurried, she'd get to buy herself a drink, if not...oh, she didn't want to think about the alternative. The only bar around that stayed open later than Leo's was the Bottom's Up on Calle Ocho, a topless bar she'd driven by countless numbers of time.

Shoes on, she climbed down the stairs, feeling severe pain. But if she got her next drink she wouldn't feel a thing...that was the way it was...drink and feel no pain, no pain at all...

છ૰ન્

18
Casa Maura

Sofía tired of waiting. She finally realized that her mother was not coming home. Laura must have stayed at her aunt's house. That was it, they went out to dinner, had little too much vino, and her mother decided not to drive home.

She waited outside the house for hours. Even contemplated breaking in, but the neighbors would call the police if they heard or saw her break one of the windows.

If she walked back to the public phone, it'd be to call a taxi to come and pick her up and take her to Casa Maura. She might just as well do that, instead of wasting any more time waiting.

The mosquitoes were driving her crazy. She felt the bumps over her legs and arms. One bit her on the forehead. Those bloodthirsty bastards she could stand, but not the *cucarachas*, the roaches, which she looked out for. They might crawl out of some crack or from under a crevice and...she shuddered at the thought. She had always hated those vermin, especially when she lived in Mexico and she and her sisters slept in the same room. They took turns looking out for them at night. Night-watch duty, they called it. If they spotted one, they screamed for their brother Samuel or for their uncle or father to come and kill the critters. Most of the time it was Samuel who rushed into the room, shoe in hand or rolled-up newspaper, found the roach, and smashed it to a pulp.

"Okay," Samuel would say. "I killed it. I am your knight in pajamas." And then they would gang up on him and kiss him, and he hated it.

Her mother was not coming home, Sofía finally convinced herself. She reached for her purse, stood up, and checked the bottom of it for American change. Any quarters among her Argentine coins?

None. That was all she needed now. Stranded. Not able to call anyone to come pick her up. She would call her cousin Celia, whom she knew was living in an apartment, but she didn't have the number. Didn't know much about her boyfriend either, and he might not like it if she called this late.

Okay, she thought, this was what she'd do. The game plan. She'd walk over to the Farm Store and plead with the man working the cash register to let her use the phone.

Why not knock at the neighbor's front door and ask if she could use the phone. They might recognize her and understand her predicament, so what if it had been a long time since she'd lived across the street?

To try won't hurt.

She walked out of the darkness of her parents' porch and into the brightness of the neighbor's front door. Had she known the time, she wouldn't have dared disturb these people, but she was desperate.

Go ahead, knock!

It took someone a long time to reach the door and ask who it was.

"Neighbor's daughter from across the street," she said.

The curtain of the side window parted and a pale face looked at her. A man's face.

"What do you want?"

She explained to the man she was stranded and would like to use his telephone.

"You know what time it is?"

She would like to know it.

The man said, "It's forty-five minutes past one in the morning. I work, young lady. Have to be up by five-thirty.

"To be honest with you," the man continued, "I've never seen you before."

"I can show you my driver's license." She had one with her parents' address on it.

The man prolonged his scrutiny of her. "All right," he said. "Go ahead, but make it quick and don't speak too loud. My wife's asleep."

She didn't remember these people either. They must have moved in after she got married and left for Buenos Aires.

The man was tall and skinny; his pajamas were too short and tight with open space between the buttons. He led the way to the phone in the dining room. The phone was one of those fake antique jobs made out of plastic.

She dialed her aunt's telephone number. Let it ring.

The man looked at her.

"I must have dialed wrong," she said. Then, "You wouldn't know a number to a taxi company?"

"Try eights," he said. "Seven eights is all you need."

"Eight," she said and dialed it quickly.

A dispatcher answered, "Address?"

She gave him her address.

"Give the driver five minutes."

She hung up and thanked the man for the use of his phone. If the cab didn't show up, she'd be sleeping on the porch, or out by the pool in the back.

"Good night," she said to the man.

He grunted something that sounded like "Good luck."

The minute she was out the door, the man turned off the porch light.

❧

The taxi finally arrived. Sofía told the driver, a gringo this time, the address of her aunt's house. She also asked the time. The man said it was 2:30 in the morning. Her mind wandered off to Buenos Aires. Surely, Ariel must have called. Eventually, he'd get the hint that something was wrong. She only hoped he panicked. A panic attack in Tokyo, that was what he deserved, in a foreign strange place, among strangers...that would teach him to be such a bastard.

At the Ferdinand address, as the taxi pulled up the driveway, all the lights were on in the house, but no sign of anyone moving about and no cars in the driveway. Sofía needed money to pay the driver.

"Can you wait?" she asked him. "I'll get the money inside."

The driver gave her a creepy smile. "Go ahead," he said. "I'll wait around."

She went up the porch steps, knocked, and then tried the knob and found the front door open.

"*Tía*," she said. "Mother!"

No answer.

She looked on top of the table for money, in the drawers. Then in the kitchen was all that broken glass. Maybe someone broke in, she thought, and that was why no one was around.

Sofía didn't know whether to stay or go. But where would she go?

An idea struck her then. She looked for her aunt's address book. She found it in the kitchen, in the drawer directly under the microwave oven. In it, she looked up Celia's number. She moved toward the phone, picked up the receiver, and dialed.

The phone rang several times and a man answered. His voice sounded sleepy. She woke him up, she thought, Celia's boyfriend.

She said: "This is Sofía, Celia's cousin." Sofía and Rafael had met once when she had visited last year.

"Hi," he said. "Where are you?"

"I'm at Casa Maura." Then she explained her predicament to him.

"Wait a sec, I'll wake up Celia."

She heard him clearly trying to stir Celia awake. Her cousin came on the line.

"Celia, it's Sofía."

"What's going on?"

"I got to your mother's and nobody's here. The front door was open and there's all this broken—"

"You're in Miami?" her cousin asked.

"I have a taxi waiting and no money to pay."

"Jump in and come over," Celia told her.

"What's going on, Celia?"

"I'll tell you when you get here."

"I'm on my way."

After getting the address, Sofía hung up. She thought: the taxi driver was going to think she was putting him on, but she had to get to her cousin's house somehow.

It was the only way she could pay the man; she had no other alternative.

☙❧

19

Last Call for Alchohol at the Bottoms Up

Maura drove to Leo's Liquor and, to her dismay, it was closed. All the lights were out. Parking lot empty. She hit the steering wheel of the car and cursed. On the verge of being frantic; she needed a drink. That left her with one option, that was if she didn't want to go to the local gas station and buy beer, but she didn't like beer. She wanted a real drink. A good stiff throat-burner of a drink.

Only one place served that kind of liquor at this hour, and that was The Bottoms Up. She made up her mind to go and relieve her thirst. Unlike at Leo's, the parking lot of The Bottoms Up was crowded with cars, from junkers to tinted-glass-window-Mercedes and BMWs.

All the men were out, but she didn't care where she quenched her thirst. That was the way she'd always been, except she never had the need to come here. She figured all she would have were a couple of shots, and if she craved for more she could pay for a bottle and take it home. Two drinks and she'd be all right. Fine.

She parked, locked up the car, and walked to the place. The pain on her feet was excruciating. She knew she was a disgrace to the family, but the family didn't exist right now. Didn't know. Could never understand. She had failed her sister. A simple request Laura asked her for, and she blew it.

Her head hurt. She felt the pressure building at the temples. Behind her eyes. A couple of drinks and…she strapped her purse tight under her arms and walked in. Yes, she was brave enough and in a bad predicament. She imagined how she must look. What a sight! Needless to say, she'd never set foot in such a place. The closest she had come had been the Tropicana Night Club in Havana. And Caesar's Palace in Vegas, but the women there knew how to keep their tops on and still make the money, or so she thought.

The place was dark, crowded with strange men and filled with smoke. The smell of cigarettes mixed with that of spilled beer, and a dozen fragrances of colognes clashed. The music blared. The beat pulsed between her ears. She wasted no time finding the bar.

Nobody looked at her, noticed her limp as she made it to the bar. On the other side, up on stage, was a dancer whose nudity offended Maura, but Maura was not here to look, but to drink and go.

Drink and go.

Next to her sat a fat man who held a beer with stubby fingers (pink in the light). During those few seconds she looked at him, he became the embodiment of disgust. Sweaty. Beady eyes. A receding hair line and what was left slicked back and tied into a pony tail. A drooling old bastard with nothing better to do with his time than come here and... No, she wasn't here to judge anybody.

The barkeep, a woman, who in better light would look much older, came over, placed a napkin on the bar and said, "Ladies' night's almost over, honey, so you get a last drink for free. What's your pleasure?" The woman spoke with a heavy sanded-down voice.

Maura had a hard time understanding the woman when the music resounded so loud out of the speakers, which hung nearby or sat at the corners of the bar by the liquor shelves. "One free drink," the barkeep told her. "On the house. What will it be?"

She chose Black Label. "No," the woman shook her head. "No. No brand names. House liquor only."

She told the barkeep she'd pay then. "Coming right up," the barkeep said.

Maura told her she wanted her drink straight. The bar-keep looked at her with a probing glance, as though she, the barkeep, knew the feeling. Maura felt the fat man's eyes on her.

Pervert, she thought, go home to your wife and children.

The drink arrived and saved her. She took a quick gulp, then another, and immediately she sensed a certain weight lift off her shoulders.

The music ended. One dancer finished her number and another stepped on to the stage. She wore a G-string and something straight out of the Fredericks of Hollywood cata-log, a silk and lace negligee.

The disc jockey said, "Now, here's Vivian for your plea-sure, gents. For your eyes only. Enjoy her, she's yours. This being the last dance and last call for alcohol, don't forget to tip your waitresses and bartender. Feel free to approach the stage and let Vivian know how thrilled you are to see her."

Maura paid for another drink, drank it down, and ordered another. The drinks had calmed her down, like she knew they would. This was a view of America she'd never cared to see before, and here she was tonight, thirst having forced her to come. It was while sitting here, caught among these strange and shady characters, a drink in her hand, still feeling thirsty, that she came to admit that she did have a problem.

She *was* an alcoholic, even when the disc jockey announced that the last dance was almost over, that this was really the last call, she went on craving, wanting, needing, and she knew she must leave before the lights came on, before all these men started to pile out on their way to their cars.

Drink up and go, she said to herself. One down, one more to go.

20
No Sleep

Wrapped in a bathrobe, Rafael's (hers was dirty), Celia waited for the taxi to bring Sofía. No way would she think about her mother's whereabouts. She was through dealing with her. On the steps of the apartment building, she looked up at Jane's window. All the lights were out except for the one in Jane's daughter's room. The daughter was probably on the phone working on new schemes, plans, Celia thought.

Mothers and daughters, Celia contemplated while she waited, what a trauma. Why couldn't most of them get along? She never got along with her mother, her overprotectiveness. Come on. She got along better with her father, but then again her father had never been in town long enough to get on her nerves. She certainly got along better with her aunt. How could two sisters be so different? But, hey, she wasn't blaming anybody. Celia needed a break. From school. From thinking about relationships. From life.

What she needed was a good long rest. Tomorrow, come morning, she was calling in sick. Fuck them all, the administration, student body, the whole shebang! She wasn't about to lose her sanity over anybody. Hell, she was too young. Fuck responsibilities, for she'd been responsible too long.

She could feel the palpitations of her heart, and it was an irregular heartbeat. Arrhythmia, they called it. Caused by stress.

Not a car coming by. No headlights. The tennis courts across the street hid in the darkness. The street light at the corner was out.

She remembered a line, a great one, from *Slaughterhouse Five* by Kurt Vonnegut. "So it goes," Billy Pilgrim always said. *So it goes*, she said now.

Celia decided not to think about schoolwork, parents, family. She wished to break through with a new identity. That of an individual. She wanted to be respected.

A car turned at the corner. A taxi. She stepped down, moved to the curb, and flagged down the driver.

Her cousin opened the door and climbed out. Sofía.

The driver told Celia the amount. $13.50. Celia reached into the pockets of the robe for a twenty and handed it to the driver.

"Give me five back," she told the man. "And keep the change."

The driver looked at her as if a dollar-fifty wasn't enough of a tip, but she didn't care. The man dropped the five on her hand and took off.

Now she got a chance to hug Sofía, who looked worn and tired. Sofía looked thin, too.

Celia assumed Sofía was here because of her father's heart attack.

"I left Ariel," Sofía said.

"No joke?"

"We are through."

"Hey, no bags?"

"One. Left it in Kendall." Then, "Where's everybody?"

"Let's go inside," Celia said.

"There was glass all over your mother's floor."

"It's a long story," Celia told her.

"We all have one."

They entered the apartment through the kitchen door. In the kitchen, where all the cabinets were painted in pastel colors, was the coffee pot filled with freshly brewed coffee. How nice of Rafael to get it going for them.

It was going to be a long night.

Wasabi and Sato came into the kitchen and rubbed against Sofía's legs. "What pretty cats," she said.

"They like you."

Sofía picked up Sato and said, "So what's going on?"

Celia told her about Zacarías. Sofía was shocked; Celia was surprised by the coincidence of her cousin arriving right when Zacarías had a heart attack. After Sofía calmed down about the news of her father, they talked about him.

"He works too hard," Sofía said. Sato wormed his way out of Sofía's arms. He joined Wasabi on the other side of the dining room.

"He'll have to slow down now," Celia added.

"You know he won't."

They both nodded and agreed that it was true. Nothing would make Zacarías stop working. He loved what he did too much.

"Sometimes," Sofía said, "I wished I could have that same kind of passion for something."

"Me too."

"It must be a great feeling, knowing that what you do isn't work because you *love* to do it."

"Your mom would love it if he retired," Celia said.

"She's been after him about that. He could lecture at a university and take it easy. But no, he's wanted to live on the go. Remember how little we saw of him when we lived in Lomas Verdes?"

"He came home on rare occasions," Celia said, "and when he did, he tried to be too strict with us."

"I hope he's all right," Sofía said. "I hate to think what it'll do to mother if—"

"He's fine, I'm sure."

Celia stood up and asked Sofía if she wanted another cup of coffee. Sofía said yes, so Celia poured. They sat down and again and continued with their conversation. Men, they both contemplated, were strange. Sofía didn't want to say much about Ariel and her two years spent with him, so to keep the conversation going while they drank coffee and became more and more awake, she asked Celia how she met Rafael.

They met about a year ago, while she was still at the university. She had sent her resume to the Dade County School District Board of Education. They told her to come down for an interview and she did. She had no idea about the high turnover of teachers. They came and went, every semester. It was right before spring break, so she figured why not? She was coming down to see her parents anyway, so why not go in?

The morning she went in for the interview, she parked the car outside the school-board building and walked down the sidewalk, where, up on a scaffolding, Rafael and three other local artists, were painting a mural. Something multicultural.

The board had commissioned the mural and was paying each ten grand. Rafael represented the Cuban-American community, and his part had to do with his heritage. Later, after she got to know him, she found out he had taken this job because he needed the money. His last art exhibit had been jinxed by a woman reporter from *The Miami Herald*. She had asked him during their interview who had influenced his art, and Rafael gave her only names of male artists—Pollock, DeKooning, Picasso, Sholder. And no women? the paper woman had asked him. Rafael told her yes. There were two: Frida Kahlo and Georgia O'Keefe. The newspaper woman wrote up a column about Rafael being a macho artist whose male perspective pervaded his images. She accused him of being a misogynist.

Needless to say, very few women attended his exhibition, and since then he held a grudge because he felt art had nothing to do with whether the artist was male or female. You used the images that came to you, that was it. You worked with whatever you could, and the most important thing was the work.

Anyway, Celia was going to her interview when Rafael dropped the can of paint he was holding, splattering yellow paint on her heels. She was wearing a long-sleeved white blouse, a navy-blue skirt and matching pumps. Real conservative to create the right impression.

She looked up at Rafael.

He found himself tongue-tied. Quickly, he clambered down the side of the scaffold and began to apologize. With the bandanna he carried in his back pocket, he knelt and cleaned her shoes, but they were ruined.

"Oh, you must let me buy you a new pair," he kept saying.

"No shoe stores in the area," she told him as a joke, a way to put him at ease. "I'm glad I didn't park my car close by."

"Jesus," he said, looking down at her spotted shoes. "I'm really sorry."

"I don't think the shoes will get me the job."

"You a teacher?"

"Will be, I'm a student. Still. I'm trying to get a job for the fall."

"Good luck," he offered.

"Maybe," she said, and walked away.

Even when she reached the door, she felt him staring at her as she walked.

Later, after they went out on a date, he confessed her legs had taken his breath away. She had perfect legs. "I'm glad I dropped that can of paint," he said.

She went in to be interviewed by a Mr. Owen, the head of personnel. Mr. Owen was fat, bald, and had a defective eye. She couldn't help but stare at the gray-film-covered eye. She became self-conscious because she kept staring at the man's eye. She felt like the protagonist of Poe's "Tell-Tale Heart".

The questions Mr. Owen asked had little to do with teaching. "Can you get to Homestead by seven?" he said. "I mean since you live in Coral Gables."

She clarified. "My parents live there; I can move closer to school."

Thank heavens she never did. The long drives had saved her. They helped to cool her off.

"Good, good," Mr. Owen told her as his one eye opened wide. "I strongly recommend that you do move closer to the school."

She felt like she had scored a lot of points by making that suggestion.

Plaques and a picture of Ronald Reagan hung behind Mr. Owen. Certificates and diplomas.

"I think you will like Homestead," he said. "It is a very pretty place. All that open land and the smell of things growing."

Then Mr. Owen looked over her resume. He nodded and smiled. "I think you are highly qualified," he said.

She knew that by listing all her education courses first, they would attract the interviewer's attention. Still, Mr. Owen didn't ask her any questions about theory or practice in teaching.

So, she decided to leave her mark. "I hear that the school in Homestead is run by school-based management." She knew about it because she had looked up the school.

This seemed to impress Mr. Owen. He gave her the awed, wide-eyed treatment again, which only made her focus on his bad eye.

"What do you know about it?"

"Teachers and administrators," she said, "as well as the principal work as a team in running the school."

"That's correct," he said.

Mr. Owen looked at her credentials one more time, then stood up. He said, "Miss Torres, welcome aboard. You've got the job."

Was it her imagination or had she just gone through the easiest interview ever? She acted surprised.

"As soon as you graduate," he said, "you come down here. We'll have a good job waiting for you."

She and Mr. Owen shook hands. The job was hers. What Mr. Owen forgot to tell her, of course, and what she found out early that fall, was that she still needed to be approved by the school-based management hiring committee. She did get approved, but those fuckers gave her a hell of a time. She remembered one of the assistant principals (there were four) who asked her, "Miss Torres, what would you do if a male student followed you home?"

That was when she knew she was going to be in trouble.

"Send him home immediately," she said. "Then report him the following morning."

"Report it to whom?"

"A counselor."

She got the job.

Back outside, after the first interview with Mr. Owen at the Board of Education, feeling excited and doubtful at the same time, she looked for the muralist.

Rafael stuck his head out of a van as she walked by and asked her how her interview had turned out.

"Got the job," she told him.

He looked at her legs and said, "Lucky shoes."

She smiled.

He came out of the van and straight out asked her for her phone number. "I'd like to buy you a pair of shoes."

"You really don't have to."

"Then how about dinner?"

She said yes to the dinner, except she had a couple of days left in town, then she had to go back to the university. They went out on their first date the night before she went back to Gainesville.

"And that," she said to Sofía, "is how I met Rafael. The rest, as they say, is history."

ঔৎ৯

21

Alone at Night in a Foreign Country

After Laura signed the release and identification forms and the death certificate in triplicate, Juan Carlos drove her to a hotel near the airport. She wasn't feeling well, but hardly showed it. What she needed was rest. On the way, Juan Carlos told her everything about all the requisites to be able to take Zacarías back to Florida.

"If there's anything you need, Laura," he said. "Please let me know."

She thanked him for all the things he'd already done, for his support and consideration

"I will have everything ready," he said. "Also, in the morning I'll come by and pick you up. Take you to the airport."

"I appreciate your help," she said.

"It's the least I could do," Juan Carlos said. Zacarías was not only his mentor, but a very good friend. He was almost like a father. Zacarías always gave him good advice. When he told Juan Carlos he should work on a Masters in Land Management because the job market was changing, becoming more and more specialized and competitive, Juan Carlos did not hesitate to enroll at the university.

"He was one of a kind, your husband," he said.

At the hotel, he helped her check in and walked her to the bedroom. He carried her only suitcase into the room, asked her where he should put it, and moved back toward the door. Once again he took her hand and told her that she had to be strong the way Zacarías would expect her to be, ready to go on with her life.

Before leaving he said, "I need a favor from you."

"Of course."

"I'd like to attend the burial."

"Certainly, Juan Carlos," she said.

"I already made the reservation," he added. "I wish I could go with you, but I have to return to the fields—to give the workers instructions in my absence. I will be in Florida Saturday morning. But I need a place to stay."

"You can stay at the house."

"It means a lot to me to be able to be there."

They said goodbye, and she closed the door as soon as he left. Her bones ached. Her feet. She needed to rest her mind.

She dialed the front desk and asked the operator to place a wake-up call for 6 a.m. She wanted to be up early to take her time. It was having to rush that made her nervous.

Removing her clothes, she sat on the bed, leaned back. She closed her eyes for a brief moment and felt so strange in this room, in this hotel, in this country... Under such circumstances, she figured, she'd feel awkward anywhere in the world.

It was hot in the room, so she looked for the air conditioner and turned it on high. Then she reached for the phone and dialed room service and ordered tea and bottled water.

In her purse she found her emergency sleeping pills. She hadn't used them in a long time, but tonight she would need all the help she could get. She'd take one pill with the tea and then go to sleep.

More relaxed now, wearing her robe which she removed from her suitcase, she stretched on the bed. Her back hurt, but the coolness of the bed seemed to alleviate the pain. While she waited for room service to bring the tea and water up, she called the operator and asked her to place a call to her sister Maura in Miami.

"Nobody answers," the operator said after making the connection.

"Keep trying, please," Laura said. "And ring me back if you get through."

She couldn't help but wonder why nobody was answering at Maura's. If Maura went on a drinking rampage, Laura knew she wouldn't get any messages to her. That fool, her younger sister.

The tea and water arrived. A young girl in a gray uniform brought in the tray and set it on the round table. Laura tipped the girl in dollars because she didn't have any *cruzeiros*. The girl accepted the money and left.

After drawing the curtains open, Laura turned off all the lights in the room and sat down to have the tea. She looked outside. It was a lovely view of the mountains in the twilight, a gridlock of lights flickering at their foothills. The lights shimmered like fireflies from this far away. Her window faced the airport, so she could see airplanes take off and land.

She would be home by tomorrow, then she could take charge of calling her children, the family, and breaking the sad news to them. As soon as she got off the plane, she must make the funeral arrangements. She and Zacarías had bought plots in Shadyhills Cemetery five years ago. The service, she decided, would be held at Ziegler and Curtis Funeral Home in Kendall, near the house. The cemetery was nearby, too. She wanted to able to take Zacarías flowers all the time.

Taking the pill, she thought of the family. How would she break the news to them? Cristina, she knew, would be devastated. She was the closest to Zacarías.

Yes, she would be there for all her daughters and her son, Laura thought.

Samuel would have to come home, decide what to do with the company, the consulting firm—Zacarías's pride and joy. His life. It was going to be tough for him to make a decision right away. She was thinking of Samuel. With Gisell, he would have to think about it, look for a way to accommodate his wife.

Norberto might want to step in and help run the company. After all, he was experienced. Maybe if he spent more time in Miami, he could help Maura recover.

She liked her tea on the bitter side, without too much sugar. With the second cup, she began to wonder if one sleeping pill would put her out. Now she yawned. In a little while the pill began to take effect.

Drinking her last cup of tea, she felt drowsy. When she looked at the blinking lights of the airplanes, they blurred. She left the table and tucked herself into bed. It was cool and soft. Before she surrendered to its comfort, her last thoughts were uneasy ones. They all related to Zacarías. What chances might have existed that he be saved.

A heart attack, she knew, was all too often fatal.

Her Zacarías.

∂∽

Cuarta

Funeral Arrangements

22
The Queen of Bitch

When Maura returned to her own house, the phone rang. She built up enough courage to answer it. She picked up slowly, listened.

"*Hola*, Maura!" It sounded like the voice of Samuel.

"Samuel?" she said.

"Maura," he said. "We're here at the airport. Can you pick us up?"

"What time is it?"

"Almost three."

"I'll be right over."

"Maura? Have you heard anything about my father?"

"No, nothing yet."

Samuel told his aunt that he and Gisell would be waiting downstairs outside baggage claim. Maura felt horrible, with a lot of pain on her feet. Nevertheless, she got back in the car and drove slowly to the airport. Even though she knew the way by heart, she tried to drive carefully for fear a cop would stop her and she'd end up in jail. If she only had a piece of gum, she thought, and regripped the steering wheel.

She drove down fifty-seventh to the perimeter, around the landing strip to the arrivals section of the terminal. Miami International had grown too big, which only pointed out how big the city had become. Always, when Zacarías or Norberto traveled, she was the one who made the trips to and from the airport.

On the lookout for Samuel and Gisell, Maura stayed to the right, holding steady. Samuel was short, with curly black hair and dark skin. He had Laura's face, but only when he didn't grow a beard.

Gisell, last time Maura saw her, had bleached her hair blond. But Gisell's looks, Maura knew, changed with her moods. She was a regular chameleon. No one knew how Gisell was going to react to anything, what nonsense she was likely to say next. Maura remembered the summer Gisell shaved her head because she wanted to know, once and for all, how many times she had busted her head open as a child.

Maura drove on and reached the very end of the terminal before she spotted her nephew. Samuel looked thin, tired. Her poor nephew. The problem was he spoiled Gisell. Maura had always loved her nephew, partly because he reminded her of her father who was gentle and giving.

"*Tía!*" Samuel shouted. "Open the trunk!"

She pulled the switch to let the trunk open. Samuel threw the bag in the trunk, came around, opened the door, and let Gisell get in first. Then he climbed in the back and kissed Maura. Gisell greeted her. She had a serious look on her face. Maura wondered what was wrong, but she didn't want to ask and be told to mind her own business.

"How are you?" Samuel said, and put his hand on Maura's shoulder.

"I've been better."

Gisell smelled the alcohol on Maura's skin, then said, "Sammy, why don't you drive?"

"I'm tired," Samuel said.

"Your aunt's probably tired, too."

"I can drive," Maura said.

Samuel wanted to know about his father.

"I haven't heard from your mother," Maura said.

Then they grew quiet. Maura sensed something awfully wrong between her nephew and his wife. A thick wall of animosity.

"I've been trying to reach your sisters," Maura lied. Well, in part; she had tried to call Sofía and she had spoken that once to Beatriz.

"Where's Cristina?" he asked.

"I don't know," Maura said. "Your mother mentioned something about Texas."

"Texas?" Gisell said. "What would she be doing in Texas?"

"Some kind of contest."

Samuel and Gisell said "Oh!" in unison.

"Did you have a good flight?" Maura asked.

"Are you kidding?" responded Samuel.

"The red-eye express was a bitch," Gisell added, remembering the man who sat next to her and gave her the creeps.

Maura wouldn't know about such flights because she didn't like to fly unless she had to. She should have gone to Brazil with her sister.

"How's work?" Maura asked her nephew.

"All right," answered Samuel.

"I don't like it," said Gisell.

Maura knew Gisell didn't like to work. Between work and boredom, Gisell would choose boredom.

"I'm hungry," Samuel said.

"Me too."

"Didn't they feed you on the plane?"

"No, Maura," Gisell said. "No food on the red eye. It's a no-nonsense flight."

"We can stop somewhere," Maura told them. "*La Carreta* is open twenty-four hours."

"I haven't eaten there in ages," said Gisell. "That'll be wonderful."

Maura thought Gisell's problem was that she exaggerated everything. She made an elephant out of an ant, as the saying went, or something to that effect. Now Samuel spoke and ruined his wife's possible enjoyment. "What if my mother calls. Or one of my sisters. If we're not there, we'll miss the call."

Gisell said nothing.

"There's a little food at home," Maura said to ease the tension. Then she remembered all the broken glass..

"Let's order take-out," Gisell suggested.

Take-out it was. From the airport they drove to *La Carreta* and ordered *vaca frita* and *ropa vieja* with *moros* and *maduros*. It took fifteen minutes to get their order filled.

Food in hand, they drove back to Casa Maura and all the broken glass on the floors.

All of them went about the kitchen carefully. Maura tried to explain all the broken glass by saying a tray had fallen off the kitchen counter. While Samuel and Gisell ate, Maura swept up the debris into a mound by the kitchen door. She wished she could go barefoot, but all the cuts would give her away. Still, it was no secret; her nephew knew about her so-called drinking problem.

As soon as they were done eating, Maura cleared the table and washed the dishes and put them on the rack to dry.

Gisell lit up a cigarette and leaned back to help her digestion.

"The food was fantastic," Samuel said. "I haven't eaten like that in a long time."

"Welcome back," Maura told them.

Samuel glanced at the last of the glass, but didn't say anything.

"Things pile up in the cupboards, in the refrigerator," Maura once again offered as a possible explanation. "But the minute you open a door..."

"That's a lot of glass," he said.

She looked at it and shrugged.

"Samuel," Gisell said. "I'm going upstairs."

"I can drive you to Kendall," Maura offered.

"We can crash here," Gisell said.

"All right," said Samuel.

That was the thing about Gisell, Maura thought. She wasted no time making herself comfortable—she was selfish and self-centered beyond belief. So Gisell went upstairs. The minute she was out of reach, Samuel looked at Maura and made a strange face, as if to say: I'm tired and I don't care about her. Suddenly, his black eyes filled with a terrible sadness, the kind of sadness Maura recognized and knew all too well, especially coming from Samuel's big beautiful eyes.

"We're not doing too well," he said. "I think it's too much trouble to keep this boat from sinking."

And what a boat it was! Maura said to herself. It was the Lusitania and the Titanic all in one, without rowboats, without life jackets. She wanted to tell him to let it sink, let Gisell go, and learn something from the experience.

Life was like that, no? Up/down. Nonsense. A lot of crap and dead ends.

"*Fuerte, ponte fuerte*, Samuel," Maura said.

Samuel washed his hands and dried them with a paper towel.

"You can sleep on my bed," she said.

"Thanks, but I'm used to the couch."

That was the right thing to do, sleep alone and let her miss you, let her do some of the work for a change. That was the problem with him, Maura thought. He was too good. Willing to forgive and forget. A relationship should be half and half, not a tug of war with the one person pulling dead weight. A young woman like Gisell had to be taught responsibility, which was the hardest thing when she had nothing but confetti for a brain. But who was she, Maura Torres, to judge? She was no ideal person, far from it. But at least she knew what her problem was.

Samuel kissed her good night and went to the bathroom upstairs. Maura heard his heavy footsteps.

Tired, she could feel the weariness herself. She had reached that point of exhaustion when the body could go no further, not even when the mind showed signs of restlessness. Yes, she too would turn in. She would get some sleep. Some rest. She turned off all the lights. Laura had not and probably would not call now.

Couth barked at something unseen from the deep dark of the yard. Maybe he barked at her. Carefully, gripping on to the handrails up the stairs, she pulled herself up. Then she slipped into bed, a tree cut down, and immediately drifted into the void that was sleep.

಄಄

23

After the Balcony Scene

Photographs chosen, developed, enlarged, printed on to 8-by-10 Kodak quality paper, and hung to dry (she'd press them on the way), Cristina checked the time and noticed that she could get a few hours of sleep. Most of the hard work was done. Having finished with their love-making on the balcony, Grace and Nubi, too, had decided to call it a night and had returned to bed.

The television was still on with the volume turned off when Cristina emerged from the dark of the bathroom, her back stiff, her fingers numb, and her eyes hurting.

She looked over at her friends. Grace's body was curled up into a fetus-in-the-womb position. Part of her back showed under the sheets. Against the dark of Nubi's flesh, her pale skin stood out. Nubi had fallen asleep with a content smirk on his face. Why wouldn't he?

Cristina fell back on the mattress, looked up at the ceiling, and told herself it was too late to try her mother again. She wanted to hear her mother's voice, to tell her about her exciting new project.

છ⊷఼

24
Pets

Sofía listened to her cousin Celia tell the story of how she met her boyfriend. A long time ago she learned to pretend she was listening, when in fact she was thinking of other things. Not necessarily more important, but other things nevertheless. Sofía kept thinking about her father. What was happening to him? Where was her mother, and why hadn't she called?

Celia. Her cousin, who'd grown up to have the prettiest dark hair, almond eyes, and small nose. Sofía remembered Celia as a crybaby. Everything bothered her. Practical jokes and pranks sent her pouting and crying. If they (all the cousins) acted mean, something children had a knack to do, Celia cried. If an arm, a leg, or the head of a doll came off while they played, this would scare Celia. She'd wail away. When they played hide-and-seek and nobody bothered to look for her, Celia gave herself away by crying her lungs out.

They all knew Maura spoiled Celia because she was an only child. Celia was made out of the finest china, so to speak. Nobody could touch her. Anything she wanted, Celia got—birds, fish, a dog, cats.

Celia always got the toys. At home she grew used to having her way, with everything and everybody. The only one who wouldn't tolerate her acting the spoiled brat was her, Sofía. She was six years older, and though she didn't play much with her cousin, they still lived in the same house in Lomas Verdes. And they lived in the same house because their parents wanted it that way.

Now Celia sat in front of Sofía and drank coffee. Celia looked happy with her new independence, with her casual lifestyle. Her boyfriend was asleep in the only bedroom.

Though the place was small, it was cozy with the natural wood furniture, the book shelves filled with oversized art books, and the aquariums. The aquariums were dark. The bubbling sounds of the pumped air breaking on the surface was soothing. Posters hung from the walls, framed in simple do-it-yourself glass and plastic frames.

That was all the furnishings they had. They also had the ornaments Zacarías brought back from Guatemala and Mexico on his frequent trips. Clay churches, candelabra, wooden, rainbow-colored fish and paper-maché figurines.

They sat by the dining room table on rattan chairs. The coffee they drank was Kona Macadamia nut blend, which tasted excellent.

Soon, Celia took a sip and sneezed. She did so three times, which startled the Siamese cats awake. The cats came out in unison from the dark hall. They stretched and yawned.

Celia told her she'd been fighting her allergies, which made her sneeze. She thought she was allergic to everything, including the coffee, but she was not about to stop enjoying things because of all her allergies.

"Maybe it's the cats that you are allergic to," Sofía told her.

"The cats, dust, lint, pollen," Celia added. "But I've had these allergies before."

Celia told her how Rafael found the cats.

"I think pets are a better alternative to having children."

Celia thought about this.

"They don't drive you crazy," Sofía continued. "Some clean after themselves." She smiled.

"Children don't have to be a nuisance," Celia said.

Sofía became pensive, then admitted, "Now, I don't think I'll be having any."

"Did Ariel want—" Celia began, then stopped.

Sofía finished for her. "Children? I'm sure he did, but he's not having them with me."

When Sofía first arrived, she didn't want to get into the details of why she and Ariel had broken up. Celia had respected her cousin's wishes.

"I wish him good luck with his new life," Sofía said to Celia, and smiled.

Celia sneezed again. The cats flinched. Sofía reached over and handed her the box of Kleenex. Celia blew her nose. They sat in silence now and enjoyed their coffees. Sofía drank all of hers, stood up, and helped herself to another cup.

"How are Rafael's paintings?" Sofía asked. "I don't see any here."

"Most of what he had here is up for exhibit," Celia added. "He's doing all right, with his art I mean, but he's had a financial dry spell."

"You guys don't seem to need much," Sofía told her. "You keep things simple."

"We go out to dinner a lot. All the restaurants in this area are extra expensive."

"I'd like to see his work," she said.

"You will. I'll give you an invitation to the opening."

The cats started to wrestle. Wasabi, the youngest of the two cats, growled in complaint.

"Sato's full of energy. He sleeps all day and bothers Wasabi at night."

"Who came up with the names?"

"I came up with Wasabi, which is the green hot spice served with sushi. Rafael named the other one after an artist friend of his."

Cats. They reminded Sofía of the litter in Lomas Verdes, and she brought it up.

Norberto had returned from a trip with a gift for Celia and her cousins. A pair of kittens. He'd picked them up on the way back from a trip through Sonora.

"Remember that?" Sofía asked.

"Sure do."

The cats grew up and had a litter of deformed kittens. Sofía found them in her closet. The formless creatures writhed and shrieked and cried. Some were missing their feet and tails. One had no eyes. And two were joined at the back. It was a gruesome sight that sent Celia crying when she saw the malformed kittens. That's how their mothers found out.

Laura immediately called the maid and asked her to get rid of the kittens. *"Pobrecitos miserables!"* said the maid as she dunked them in a tin bucket full of water and held them under until they stopped wiggling in her hands. Afterwards she buried them in a deep hole in the backyard, then put rocks and bricks on the grave so that the wild dogs wouldn't dig them up.

When Norberto returned to Mexico City, he took both cats with him and let them loose in another neighborhood.

"It took awhile for him to tell us what he had done with the cats," Sofía said.

"My father's always been a practical liar."

To change the conversation, Sofía said, "That seems like such a long time ago. Those days in Lomas Verdes."

"They are," Celia said.

"And Beatriz is going back over there. I can't believe it."

"She's not going to live in Lomas Verdes though."

"I know. Acapulco's different."

"Maybe the whole family will be together then. Do you remember the last time we all got together?"

"Not since Mexico."

Always during the holidays or for special family events, either her uncle or her father and sometimes both at the same time were not in town. They often missed graduations, birthday parties, most of their daughters' Holy Communions. They always missed Thursday dinner, Celia thought.

"Yes, it's been years," she said.

"It's kind of funny how that goes," Sofía said. Then, "I'm back and Beatriz is going to live in Mexico. I'm getting divorced; she married. Strange."

Celia smiled but didn't say anything, perhaps because she didn't want to be asked the mandatory question: when was she getting married?

"I want to find a place like this one," Sofía said.

"Won't you stay in Kendall?" Celia asked.

"For a while, but then, once I start to work or going to school, I want to live on my own. I need more privacy," Sofía answered.

Celia understood. Privacy was the strongest bond between a family, no matter how small or large. Her mother invaded her privacy every chance she got. Looked through her purse, her pants, clothes in the closet. She snooped and drank, spent months doing that.

One afternoon Celia got home and found Maura looking through her purse. She startled her mother, who dropped the evidence on the floor. Her birth control pills.

"Now you know I'm not a saint," she had told her mother.

Maura walked out of the room. She didn't speak to her daughter for days, then she wrote her a note apologizing and left it on the bed. That was the way they communicated after an argument of such magnitude. With notes.

Instead of becoming more awake, the coffee and so many pauses in their conversation, which had gone well into Friday morning, had the opposite effect on the cousins. Sofía yawned, then Celia.

"You can sleep on the sofa bed," Celia told her cousin. "If the cats bother you, push them away."

Celia found her an extra comforter in the hall closet, just in case Sofía got too cold with the air conditioner on and dropped it on the sofa bed along with a sheet and a pillow.

Sofía asked at what time Celia went to work.

"I'll call in sick," Celia said.

"Maybe," Sofía said, "we'll hear something about my father soon."

"We will."

Once the sofa bed was made, the cousins said good night. Sofía listened to the building settling, the squeaks and creaks in the pipes and walls, while she removed her clothes. She put on a long T-shirt Celia gave her and got in bed.

The spring mattress felt hard. She still had a lot on her mind, especially about her father's well being, but she was exhausted. What a trip this had been so far, she thought. And it was far from being over.

☙❧

25

Dawn, Next Day

The wake-up call startled Laura. She opened her eyes to an intense, bright light. She left the curtain wide open, and now the morning light flooded the room. Feeling a little rested, clearer of mind, she got out of bed and went to the bathroom. She would shower, dress, pack her things, and go to the hotel restaurant to have coffee and a cigarette while she waited for Juan Carlos to pick her up.

She faintly remembered the telephone ringing after she went to sleep. The sleeping pills helped put her out. Had she missed a call from Maura?

Deciding to try again, she left the bathroom and dialed the operator. The operator greeted her and put the new call through.

Laura heard the phone ring at her sister's house. Then on the seventh ring, Maura picked it up. "Maura," Laura said. "What happened to you yesterday? I counted on you. I depended on you being there. You told me that you'd be there and handle everything. What happened?"

"You don't want to know," Maura told her. Then, "How's Zacarías?"

Laura let the silence answer on her behalf.

"Laura?" Maura said.

"Zacarías is dead. He died by the time I got here."

She heard Maura clear her throat and begin to weep. Laura had a hard time controlling herself, tried not to...

"I'm returning this morning," Laura told her sister.

"I'll be there—what time?" Maura said.

Maura informed her that Samuel and Gisell had arrived.

"What do I tell the children?" Maura asked.

"Tell them the truth," Laura said. "Tell them Zacarías is dead."

"How about the arrangements," her sister said. "The funeral—"

"I'll take care of all that."

"I'll do as you say."

"Maura?"

"Yes."

"I need you," Laura said, "Please stay sober."

Maura greeted this with silence, which Laura took to mean that she wasn't in the mood for sermons. Well, she wasn't going to lecture her or offer advice. Maura was an adult, and Laura intended to treat her as such.

"I'll be home soon."

"I think Samuel suspects the worse."

"Is he awake?"

"Not yet."

"Don't wake him."

"I'm thinking about you," Maura said.

"Stay sober, *mi hermana*. I need you."

They said good bye and hung up.

Laura showered, brushed her teeth without looking at herself in the mirror (if she looked, she'd break down), and dressed. Once her bag was packed, she went downstairs to the front desk and checked out. Now she could wait for Juan Carlos.

In the café she sat by an open window and ordered coffee and cream. Maybe Juan Carlos would sit down and have some, too. She needed company, for she figured that if she kept her mind focused, it would not stray toward bad thoughts, thoughts of having to live without Zacarías.

She never figured that Zacarías would die of a heart attack. She often worried that he'd be kidnapped by guerrillas in El Salvador or Nicaragua and held for ransom money no one had. Or that his plane would crash and explode.

Juan Carlos arrived. He looked rested, dressed in a white short-sleeved cotton shirt and black slacks.

"Did you manage to sleep at all?" he asked and sat down.

"Thanks to a sleeping pill."

"I've taken care of everything," he said, and opened the cloth napkin and placed it across his lap. "The transportation."

The waiter guessed that Juan Carlos might be having coffee and brought another cup. He poured the steaming coffee carefully.

"Have you decided what to do?"

She told him about Ziegler and Curtis in Kendall. They would arrange the funeral, wake, and burial.

"Are you ready to order?" the waiter asked.

She opted for the continental breakfast.

Juan Carlos ordered three eggs scrambled, ham, and toast. Something to get his mind back on track.

The waiter picked up the menus and excused himself.

The coffee was cool now, and Juan Carlos drank his fast.

While they waited for their food to arrive, he remembered Zacarías's last morning on this world, and how he'd had a troubled sleep. "He thought he heard the sound of a bird," Juan Carlos said.

"A bird?"

"He was dreaming."

To know the details of her husband's last morning pleased her, but she didn't linger upon them for fear she might cry.

When the food arrived, she and Juan Carlos ate in silence, he devouring his eggs and ham, leaving only the edges of his dark toast. After one more cup of coffee each, they got ready to depart for the airport. He paid the bill, walked her to the lobby to pick up her suitcase, and then outside, opened the door of a taxi so she could climb in. They rode to the airport listening to the low Brazilian music coming from the taxi's radio.

She stared out the window at the streets riddled with children, dark-skinned boys, shirtless, wearing shorts and no shoes. Over them loomed the giant billboards and ads. Clotheslines connected the endless yards. Curtains flowed and spilled out of windows.

"I have never been here before," she said.

"It's a lovely country," Juan Carlos said.

"I hate to say it," she added, "but I don't think I will ever return."

"I understand," Juan Carlos said, then tapped the driver on the shoulder and told him to be on the lookout for the American Airlines terminal.

At the airport, Juan Carlos paid the taxi driver, carried Laura's suitcase to the check-in counter, and gave the young woman in charge the ticket. Then he handed an envelope with folded papers to Laura and said, "These are all the forms and permits you will need." He paused. "Zacarías's body will arrive in the afternoon. Once you make contact with the funeral home, they will meet the plane and move him."

Cadaver, body, was all that was left, she thought.

They walked to the gate past the security checkpoint. On another piece of paper he jotted down the time and the hour his flight arrived on Saturday.

"I have to get back to Latinia," he said.

"Thank Castello for me," she told him.

"I will."

Juan Carlos wished her a good trip and left. The flight began to board. She let people walk in ahead of her. Having a first-class ticket, she could board any time she liked. She imagined that Zacarías was travelling with her. In spirit. He was returning home to rest. Finally, she boarded the plane, found her seat, leaned back, and closed her eyes.

Homeward bound.

The plane left the gate then taxied to the end of the strip, the take-off point. The engines revved up to a high pitch. The aircraft pushed forward.

"Ladies and gentleman, we've been cleared for take off," the captain's voice came over the intercom.

The plane picked up tremendous speed and hurled itself at the sky. The sonic boom penetrated the cabin. It was in the air, she thought, floating, and it was taking her back home.

ৡৎ

26

Sick Call

The alarm buzzed at 5:30. Since it was on Celia's side, she reached over and slapped the snooze bar. Rafael stirred next to her and said, "Time to get up?"

"I'm calling in sick," she said, and groped for the phone on the floor by the side of the bed. The numbers lit up when she picked up the receiver. She dialed the substitute office number. The phone rang too loud so she moved it away from her ear until she heard someone answer.

"Good morning," she said. "This is Miss Torres. I am sick and will not be coming in today."

"Miss Torres, yes," the other person said. "Did you leave lesson plans?"

"They are in the ninth-grade office," she said.

"Hope you feel better."

Celia thanked the woman and hung up. Soon she'd be calling in sick for the rest of her life. No more schoolwork. No more teenagers in need of cool and understanding. Acceptance. No more I'm-so-confused-nobody-cares-about-me bullshit. She'd be free from all that. So what if she lost the great benefits and all the time off. She wanted her life back. She needed a normal job she could leave at the office come quitting time.

Rafael had gone back to sleep. She heard his regular breathing (sometimes he snored, but she'd never told him.) He slept with an arm over his face, as if to protect his eyes. His mouth was open with spittle at the corner of his mouth.

Come on, she told herself as she closed her eyes and tried to go back to sleep. The alarm was off. Then she realized what the problem was. Her nasal passages were clogged. She breathed through her mouth. What was she going to do about this congestion?

She blew her nose, but no air got through and her ears popped. All right, she'd breathe through her mouth. Anything to go back to sleep.

A while later she woke from a dream. What was she dreaming about? Celia turned onto her side and stared at the odd shapes floating in the dark aquariums. Focusing on the rhythm of the water flowing from the filters, she closed her eyes and waited.

It was no use, couldn't go back to sleep. She decided to get up and take her decongestant medicine and have something for breakfast. She was very hungry; her stomach grumbled the instant she thought of breakfast.

She got up, put on her robe, and walked out to the bathroom. She remembered Sofía was sleeping in the living room. Celia tiptoed to the bathroom.

In the living room, Sofía slept bundled under the comforter. It was cold, so Celia turned off the air conditioner.

In the kitchen, she started breakfast. She let the light in by rolling up the shade. When she did, she spotted a young man sitting in a red car across the street.

Then there was the sound of Jane's apartment door opening and closing. Someone went down the stairs, and then Jane appeared, dressed ready for work, and the young man in the car ducked below the partly opened tinted car window.

He waited for Jane to get in the car, start it, comb her hair, and check her make-up in the rearview mirror. After Jane drove away, the young man got out of his car, locked it, and hurried across the street and entered the building. Celia heard him hurrying up the stairs.

Jane's daughter let him in. Silence.

Celia imagined the young girl embracing her boyfriend, kissing him, that sneaky son of a bitch.

Which part of the house were they most likely to go at it, screw themselves silly?

Perhaps in the kitchen. At that age any place would do. Ah, teenagehood. Teenagedom? Boys couldn't regulate their hormones; girls got horny all the time. They'd pay for the consequences if...Celia could almost hear it. Jane said, "You will have to take responsibility now."

Crying, Meredith would sob and plead for something to be done about her growing condition. She didn't want to be a mother. But why was Celia thinking about this. Meredith was probably on BC pills.

The smell of the bacon and the eggs brought Rafael to the kitchen. "What a smell, umm!" he said.

"Want some?"

"You bet."

He came over and kissed her on the forehead. "I thought you called in sick."

"I did."

"What are you doing up?"

"Couldn't sleep."

Now Celia told him about Meredith sneaking in her boyfriend.

"I've known about it. I told you she was doing so."

"It's not fair to Jane."

"Speaking of the devil," Rafael said, and signaled at the window.

Jane was back. She must have forgotten something. Celia liked to believe Jane came back because she suspected her daughter was up to no good.

"Trouble," Celia said.

"Fandango time," Rafael said, and laughed.

They stopped to listen.

Jane went upstairs and a couple of minutes later she reappeared, got in the car again, and drove away. Nothing happened.

"Wow," Rafael said.

"She hid him."

"Crafty, aren't they?"

Sofía woke up. Celia peeked out of the kitchen and saw that the bed was empty. She approached the bathroom door. Tapping gently, she asked her cousin, "Want breakfast?"

"Sure," Sofía said. "I'll be right out."

"Take your time," Celia told her. "This is not a workday."

She returned to the kitchen to find Rafael nibbling on a bacon strip.

"Wait, let's all eat together."

"It's good."

"Put some pants on," she told him. "Sofía's here."

"She's got something against underwear?"

"She might faint if she catches a glimpse of yours."

He left her and went to the bedroom to get dressed. After a while, as she served the eggs and separated the bacon strips evenly among the three plates, the door opened and closed upstairs.

Meredith and her boyfriend stepped out with beach towels over their shoulders. Their hair was wet. Meredith wore shorts over her bathing suit. She was carrying a cooler. He had his arm around her.

He opened the door for her then took the cooler and put it in the trunk with the towels.

They drove away with the radio blaring.

Sofía and Rafael came to the dining room and sat down. Celia put the plates on the table and joined them. This was the first time they had ever had company for breakfast. In fact, it was the first time that she and Rafael had eaten breakfast together on a weekday.

The cats rubbed themselves against Celia's legs.

She ate while Sofía and Rafael talked about Zacarías and his condition. They would hear something soon.

ই৵৶ঌ

27

Gisell in the Morning

The light from an overcast morning seemed dull behind the blinds in the bedroom.

She opened her eyes slowly and looked at the popcorn ceiling, at the brown-rust stain that formed a strange image of a face.

Also, a long-legged mosquito, a giant defying gravity by lingering upside down. It hung directly over her.

Open mind. Clarity of thought.

This was what she hated about the morning.

This was (had been) Celia's room, and traces of her remained in the room. Stuffed animals, adolescent books, knickknacks brought as gifts from all over Latin America.

There were pictures on the walls of Celia as baby. Cute little girl, dreamy eyes, long straight hair, and those perfect eyebrows.

Gisell liked Celia.

Celia, she thought, liked her.

She wished she had eyebrows like that, but it made little sense to consume her energies this morning on all the things she lacked.

The pitter-patter of the rain against everything outside echoed in the room.

The rain...cooled everything.

Then the sun would come out and the humidity would be unbearable.

Frogs sounded their distant croaks of pleasure under the rain.

Miami—she was home, this was where she wanted to be. This was where she belonged.

Intended to stay.

Where was Sammy?

She was back in the same room that started all the troubles with the family. Between her and them.

Five years ago. She remembered.

She never forgot these things, which was another of her troubles.

Sammy got drunk at a party given by Norberto and Maura. Casa Maura was crowded. Noisy with salsa and merengue music. Everybody smoked and talked over the music.

She met Sammy during her year in New Orleans, at Tulane University, because he was attending the University of Florida and the Gators were in Baton Rouge to play against the Tigers. But he and his friends had gotten only as far as New Orleans—their car broke down—and she met him at Pat O'Brian's, each drinking Hurricanes, and Sammy attracted her attention because he fell into the water fountain and made a scene.

She was standing next to him when he fell and splashed water on her. Later, while he apologized, he asked her where she was from, and when she said Miami, his eyes went big and he smiled.

He gave her a great big hug, one of those she'd since seen him give other people while totally smashed. A sentimental hug, as if they had known each other all their lives, when she was a perfect stranger.

Miami.

But back to Casa Maura and the night of the party (she dropped out of Tulane). Sammy was all over her. Groping. Hanging on. He asked her to take him upstairs. He needed to use the bathroom.

He told her he didn't want to throw up in front of all the people.

When they reached the upstairs, he pulled her into Celia's room. This same room she was in now, in bed. They started to make out.

Norberto came up and found them. He caught Samuel with her breast in his hand. She saw Norberto's face ripen with anger.

That was all it took.

Norberto exploded.

He shouted at them. His voice thundered over the pulsating noise of the music and chit-chat downstairs.

"Get out!" he screamed. "Both of you."

To Sammy he said that he, Samuel, should be ashamed of his lack of respect—how could he, Samuel, fornicate on his cousin's bed?

"We are not for-for-fornicating," Samuel stuttered.

Fornicating, she had learned the true meaning, the act involved, of that word.

"I want you to take her out of here," Norberto said. "I want her out of this house. Immediately!"

"It's not her fault."

"I don't care. I don't want her in my house."

"If she goes," said Sammy, "I go, too."

"Bon voyage!"

"*Tío*, you're over-reacting."

"I saw what I saw."

"We wanted privacy."

"Seek it someplace else. Not in my house."

After this, her reputation among the members of Sammy's family became blemished, not because of their having been caught "fornicating," but because Norberto told Zacarías that he didn't approve of Sammy's choice of women.

Zacarías, too, disliked her, as she found out later, for different reasons.

"You are a loudmouth *chusma*," Norberto told her.

Chusma roughly translated into floozy.

She always knew, even now, that Sammy's sisters talked behind her back.

Screw them all, the little prissies. Prim and proper when they wanted to be.

They got laid, too, when they felt the itch. Who didn't?

All right, she thought, stop thinking about unpleasant moments and begin to plan something for the near future.

A job, she needed one if she planned to stay.

First, she would take a bath and get the grime from the trip off her skin, then she could think about it over breakfast.

28
A View of the City

Beatriz couldn't believe how much the city had grown. It spread out into the foothills. Cuernavaca had become a suburb of Mexico City. Her grandiose city. What had happened to it? To the people? Why were they swarming to the metropolis?

She thought about the probable reasons as her flight shot upward into the coffee-stain colored sky. The plane rose above the grime, achieving cruising altitude. As she looked out the oval-shaped window, the city unfolded—the metropolis, the buildings and houses ended and the patches of green and brown earth began. Patchwork, that was what the earth looked like from this high up, a giant quilt work.

Lorenzo had told her that there were almost twenty-five million inhabitants in the city now, all trying to make a living. A new servitude had arisen. Men did almost anything for gringo cash. That wicked dollar. They got you anything at any time from anywhere. Taxi drivers would take you to the moon if they could.

She flew over mountains, long arid valleys. The sun reflected off the wings. She was flying over land. She flew over rivers, over the ocean. She was flying home to Miami.

The truth was flying made her uncomfortable unless she could sit by the window and look out, even when all she could see were the cloud formations. Sometimes the earth. All that blue sky seemed so peaceful. Endless. The clouds looked like cotton balls.

She and Lorenzo had said goodbye in a hurry. Her plane was departing when they got to the airport. She almost didn't make it, and she needed to be on this flight.

When she and Lorenzo got married, they were going to move to Acapulco, to new possibilities and cleaner air. To an officer's house on the naval base. She'd visited the base before. His parents vacation at a general's house. Their house would have a view of Acapulco Bay, a piece of beach that was kept cleaner than the hotel beaches. There she would work at perfecting her tan, for, after all, she was a native. While Lorenzo sailed, she would have all the time in the world to rest and relax.

She'd be able to see the sailing ship, The Cuauhtémoc, sail in and out of the harbor, even though Lorenzo would no longer be on that ship. He was being transferred to a destroyer which guarded the coast between Mexico and Guatemala.

The sun became bright and intense. The captain of the airplane came over the intercom speakers and announced that they had left Mexico City, and at the present cruising altitude and speed, should arrive in Miami in exactly two hours and forty minutes.

Her mind drifted to last night with Lorenzo. She couldn't wait for them to be married, so that she could take him every time she pleased, without having to worry about privacy, about what people might say or think. Oh, those dark looks of his.

❧

The flight from Mexico City arrived under the rain in Miami. The temperature was in the high eighties. *Como siempre*, no? she thought, that was what she hated about the city. At its worst, it was like a sauna. Sure, there was sunshine, but not as often as people thought. There were days when it rained all morning and then the sun came out. The humidity then was unforgiving.

She called her aunt's house. Maura answered the phone.

"I'm here," Beatriz said.

"I'll be there. Wait on the median."

"What have you heard about my father?"

"Your mother's on her way back."

"How is he?"

"Let her tell you."

It dawned on Beatriz that her father had died."

After hanging up on Maura, Beatriz picked up her bag and left the coolness of the air-conditioned terminal for the infernal heat and humidity of the outside.

Suddenly, she found herself sweating, and she didn't know if it was because of the heat or because she had the premonition that her father was dead.

The heart attack killed him, she thought while she waited for her aunt to pick her up and take her home.

❧

29

Home at Last

Laura was back in Miami. She had arrived home, back to a world familiar to her. This was her territory. Samuel, Maura, and Beatriz were there to greet her even though she had asked them not to. The moment she saw them, she regained her composure.

From the look on her face, she imagined, they were able to tell she brought them bad news about Zacarías.

Beatriz was the first to ask about her father.

Laura waited an instant, swallowed, and embraced her daughter. Beatriz wept. Her brother fought back the tears swelling up in his eyes. Maura had no one but herself to lean on.

On the way home to Kendall (Maura suggested that since Juan Carlos would be arriving shortly, that Laura leave him the car here at the airport), Laura told them the details of Zacarías's heart attack and death.

She tried to give them some kind of rationale, order, the way of nature, intricate or simple as it sometimes seemed. Nature, she understood, must be allowed to take its course.

"We should have a doctor do an autopsy here," Samuel suggested. "To be sure."

"No," Laura said to her children and sister. "We must lay him to rest."

At home, they found a suitcase behind the crocuses by the door. They wondered whose suitcase it was. Samuel checked the tag. There was no name on it, no indication where the suitcase came from. He took the suitcase inside the house and said that perhaps they should try to open it and see what was inside. That might give them a clue. But the combination locks wouldn't open.

After a short rest on the living room sofa, Laura drank the camomile tea Beatriz made for everyone. It helped the nerves.

Samuel sat silent on an armed chair and pensively looked at nothing.

"Has anybody tried to reach Sofía and Cristina?"

"I tried Sofía," Maura admitted. "Nobody answers in Buenos Aires."

"Samuel, can you try her again?"

Samuel got up to make the call. When Beatriz came and sat down next to her, Laura took her hand. "How's Lorenzo and his family?"

"They are all fine," Beatriz said. "I should call and tell them."

"Let's try to reach Cristina first."

Maura told her that the best thing to do, since Cristina was on the road, was to call the college and leave her a message. Laura thought that was a good idea. Her sister was thinking. Maura wanted to help, make up for what she had failed to do yesterday.

Maura excused herself and left for the kitchen where they heard her dropping ice cubes into a glass.

"I'll call the college," Beatriz said. "What is she doing there?"

Laura told her.

"She go alone?"

"No, with Grace and Grace's boyfriend."

"When did they leave?"

"Day before yesterday."

"They should be there by now."

"Corpus Christi, Texas."

Samuel returned and said that nobody answered at Sofía's.

"She couldn't have gone to Tokyo with Ariel," Laura said. "She would have called to tell me."

"Maybe she tried."

The phone rang and Maura picked it up in the kitchen. It was Sofía calling. She was here in Miami at Celia's apartment. The suitcase belonged to her. She and Celia were on the way. Celia didn't go to work.

They were all gathering, slowly but surely. So many things that needed to be done, Laura contemplated, but her children helped. She still needed to call Ziegler and Curtis funeral home and arrange everything with them.

The wake would be held Sunday, and Zacarías would be put to rest on Monday. He would finally rest on a workday.

Finally, Beatriz got on the phone to the college in Corpus Christi and left a message with the journalism department for her sister to call home A.S.A.P.

ॐ∞ॐ

30

On the Road to Corpus Christi

They were almost there. Cristina liked the name of the city. Nubi translated it into the Body of Christ, which he pronounced the "Body of Chraaist." Grace told him to put more T into it, as in Christ! T. They passed Matagorda Bay. The view was spectacular. The sea and the sky vanished into the horizon. All the car windows were open, and the breeze that blew in carried the sting of salt.

Onward. Past the bridge that divided Copano Bay from Aransas Bay. On the map, Highway 35 zig-zagged on down to Corpus Christi. Once past Corpus Christi Bay, they entered the city limits. Welcome. Though Nubi said he was tired, legs numb, and hungry, he gave them the final push into Del Mar College, the East Campus between Baldwin Boulevard and South Staples. The map had led them in the right direction thus far.

At one of the entrances to the college, Grace asked for directions to the school of journalism. The security guard looked down at her and pointed them in the right direction.

Nubi drove around until they spotted a modern building with round glass windows, exposed painted I-beams, and a park. They left everything in the car.

They found the department, and Cristina spoke to the secretary about registering.

"What's your name?" asked the secretary.

Cristina noticed the Texas twang in her voice.

She told the secretary her name.

"Oh, I have a message for you," the woman said while she returned to her desk to fetch it. She looked into her message book and tore out the slip. Handed it to Cristina.

It was a message from Beatriz: "Call home A.S.A.P. Urgent."

"May I use the phone to make a collect call?"

"By all means," said the secretary. "Dial nine out."

Cristina dialed nine and then the operator. She asked the operator to place the call. The operator got Sofía on the line and asked her whether she accepted the call from Cristina Torres.

"Yes."

"What's going on, Sofía?"

"You must come home, Cristi," her sister said. Sofía had always called her Cristi.

"What happened?"

"Daddy died."

Cristina leaned against the secretary's desk Her lips went dry. Her head spun. She felt her blood pressure drop as if she were riding the steep fall of a roller coaster.

She asked what happened to her father.

"Heart attack."

"Oh, God, when did it happen?"

Sofía gave her all the details unsparingly. Blow by blow, the way their mother had recounted them.

Grace noticed the pale look on Cristina's face and rushed over.

"Cristina, what?"

"My father's dead."

"Oh, no," Grace said.

"I'm on my way," Cristina told Sofía.

"Hurry back. We are all here."

"I'm flying home right away."

"Goodbye."

"So long, Sofía."

They hung up.

"What are you going to do?" Grace asked.

"You guys drop me off at the airport."

What now?

"I don't know," Cristina told her friends.

"Nubi and I can frame the pictures and enter them."

"Come on," Nubi said. "We can talk about that on the way."

They hurried back to the car, and while Grace looked up the way to the airport on the map, Nubi drove them there fast.

॰॰॰

Quinta

Wake

࿇

31

The Real M

Madre. Matriarch. Mama. Mom. Mother. Queen Mother, as her husband Papi Torres used to call her. Eleonor received her summons via the granny/sitter/housekeeper/maid who answered the telephone. It wasn't that she couldn't hear, no. She found it harder and harder each day to be able to move. Laura drove over and told her the bad news.

Zacarías, her beloved son, died of a heart attack in Brazil.

Why was she the last one to find out these things? Why did her daughters-in-law do this to her? Keep her ill-informed. To try to protect her from grief? Maura might have told Laura to go easy on her. "Go easy on Eleonor's heart," she imagined Maura saying. "She's too old to handle emotional upheavals."

Oh, her son. This was not the way things were supposed to work out. She, Eleonor was to die first—wasn't that the law of nature, to allow for the old to die first? The news upset her, of course, but what upset her most was that there no longer seemed to be any order to the world. Gone was her boy Zacarías and it wasn't fair.

Eleonor was tired of those two *embusteras*, those tricksters, and all the things they kept from her. Those tricksters. They were always lying to her. Zacarías, her son, was dead. What could she do about it now? It didn't do any good to pray for his soul.

At her age (she'd lost track of the years), she'd buried all her friends, her husband, and now a son. She never intended to outlive her loved ones. Never intended to live this long. She was like an American car, not the ones being made now, but from the forties and fifties. She'd been built to last, but for how long Jesus...how long?

...a heart attack.

She had warned her son about the greasy and spicy foods. He wouldn't listen to her. That was the thing about children, you had to let go once they grew up and started treading out their own paths. Let go and hope for the best, and then these terrible things happened, which tested her faith in everything.

If she looked at the situation, she must look at it from a hopeful point of view—her son didn't have to endure living anymore. It was over.

So Laura, after giving Eleonor some time to prepare herself emotionally, called her again and told her to get dressed, that the wake was today. Of course, Laura told her, she was not expected to stay up all night. *El desvelo* was bad for someone her age. All Eleonor had to do was say the word and somebody'd bring her back to the house.

Her lovely cell. This was the prison and that damned maid was her warden.

Always somebody, never anyone in particular, Eleonor thought about what Laura told her. Early on, she knew she had become a burden. A heavy weight nobody wanted to carry. Shortly after Papi Torres died—he used to insult her by calling her his roommate— Eleonor became this thing nobody wanted to deal with.

The children grew up around their other grandmother, whom they loved more. She, Eleonor, never got a chance to play the role, for the children lived in Mexico City. How often did she get the chance to travel? By the time she could have been a grandmother to them, they had grown up. Young adults didn't care too much about grandmothers, especially the other one they didn't know.

So now they all treated her indifferently and gave her the cold shoulder. The yes-we'll-see-you-sometime treatment. All teeth and smiles. But that was quite all right because she didn't need anyone. She lived alone and liked it. Loneliness became bearable after one learned to accept it. The peace and quiet.

Besides, she was getting ready for her own departure. She thought of the long list of ailments she carried with her: bad eyesight, weak lungs, arthritis, no appetite (her taste buds no longer worked properly), recurrent kidney and urinary infections, migraines, bone and muscle aches.

She was ready indeed. Whenever her time came, she'd be ready and willing.

A long life was no good, see. A fast, happy, blissful, short one was better. But she chose this life, to be married, to be a family woman. She chose a husband, a house, some kind of stability or a semblance of law and order. Checks and balances, she called it.

Laura called to tell her somebody would be picking her up to attend her son's wake. Yes, Eleonor understood. The last time she saw her son Zacarías he looked well. Healthy and full of life. A little gut, but that was from over-indulgence. He came alone to visit her, as usual. How was everyone else? she always asked him in those general terms so he could get the hint. "Doing their own thing," he often answered. "You know how that is."

"And how are you, son?"

"Busy, mother."

He was always very busy, being a man full of hopes and aspirations. For Zacarías, every day presented itself as a new chance filled with wonderful possibilities. She reminded him that he worked too hard, and that as far as she was concerned, life was not meant to be wasted on all that work.

Zacarías said she didn't understand. Same claim Papi Torres often made.

This was what Papi Torres always believed: work hard and you will be rewarded.

What was there to understand?

Oh, Zacarías, her son, was dead.

The last time he came was in January. As usual he brought her flowers. Jasmine. She had her cataracts then, hadn't been operated on yet, and she couldn't see the colors too well. But the flowers smelled sweet. He came alone and told her he couldn't stay too long. As if he ever could.

Zacarías inherited his good looks from his father. The shiny hair, the fair skin. She remembered Papi Torres slicked his back when brilliantined hair was in fashion. Also, the friendly look in his eyes, that too came from his father. He had a sweet smile everybody liked. Perhaps it was the smile that made her son so successful. Everybody trusted Zacarías. Papi Torres had everything but the smile, so what he achieved he did so through know-how and perseverance. But she wasn't belittling Zacarías. No, not at all. Her son also had the know-how and expertise. But the smile, the ability to charm, was an extra nicety.

She would always remember her son as a baby. Of the twins, Zacarías was born first. She didn't know that she was having twins. Back then they didn't have the technology they had now. A minute or so after Zacarías opened his eyes to the world, she gave birth to Norberto, her real pride and joy.

Eleonor realized that even though she didn't disguise her favoritism well, Zacarías did not love her any less for it. The way she saw it was that Zacarías had everything: looks, intelligence, and Norberto had her.

She readied herself for her son's wake to pay her motherly tribute to him. She still had Norberto. Now she'd make a real effort to look after his health.

Zacarías was a good son. He always respected his parents. He behaved well, even as a child. He never threw tantrums, unlike Norberto. At school, he succeeded because he was among the smartest of the children.

He was a good husband. The only woman he loved was Laura, always Laura. Throughout the span of so many years, Laura—he loved her to the point of obsession.

Zacarías was a good father, though he really didn't spend that much time with his children. Whenever he came back from a long trip, he treated them all with equal love and affection. When he was in town, Zacarías spent the weekends with his family. Some Saturdays he came and visited his mother.

It seemed to Eleonor that from early on, Zacarías knew what he wanted, and that if he worked hard enough, he'd get it. He was a true professional. This was something he learned from his father. Papi Torres always told his sons that there were too many businessmen out in the world, cheap fly-by-night swindlers and charlatans, but that real, true professionals were hard to find.

The time had come for her to go to the wake, but she wasn't ready. She hadn't realized that all this time she had been remembering she had been crying. Crying over her son, taken too young from her.

☞✌

Samuel, her grandson and carrier of the Torres name, came and picked her up. He was sad, sullen, and scared. Eleonor saw it in his eyes and heard it in his voice. He was at the age when mortality became a fact of life. They hugged each other for a long time.

The boy kissed her and led her to the car. He didn't say much, except that he found her looking very well and strong. She wanted to hear more, but Samuel had a tendency to disappoint her in ever so many ways.

Well and strong, she thought, maybe ten years ago. On the outside she looked healthy, she imagined. But who knew what games her organs were playing on her this very minute?

"I am an ancient woman," she told him.

Samuel kept quiet. He pulled the seat belt about her chest, and made sure she was fastened in her seat. Then he climbed in the car and drove off.

"Where are we going?"

"The funeral home," Samuel said.

"Yes, I know. But where? Which one?"

"Ziegler and Curtis."

That was where they held the wake and funeral cere-
monies for Papi Torres.

"Is everybody there?"

"Everybody except for Cristina."

She asked where her granddaughter was.

"She stayed at home," Samuel informed her. "She got
back from a trip to Texas."

"She's not at her father's funeral?"

"No."

"That's preposterous."

"She doesn't feel well."

See what she meant? She was never told anything about
the family. The private things. Maybe, if she had been told
about Cristina, she could have gone over to the house to see
her and talk her into going to her father's funeral. Cristina
was her favorite of her grandchildren.

Once in a while they acted nicely, her family, and picked
her up to attend a dinner or a birthday party. But now she
was on her way to her son's wake, and this was a right
nobody could deny a mother.

࿇

32

A Few Words from Gisell about Pain & Grief

In-fucking-tense!

&

33
Slides & Stills

Cristina was afraid to see her father laid out in the coffin. She didn't want to see his face pale and made up. No, she detested the whole idea. Funerals, wakes, burials—she didn't want to be any part of it. After Papi Torres had died, she had made a promise never to attend another funeral, and it didn't mean she had no love or respect for her father.

She decided she was not going to attend the wake when she arrived in town. She preferred to be alone in the house in Kendall. Sure, she was all for the family sticking together during difficult and trying moments like this, but she wanted to be left alone to think and to relish the memory of her father as she knew him in life, not in death. She could do without the comforts of company.

The only weeping and crying she wanted to see and hear was her own. She took a hot bath; this was good for her nerves. And she brought back her father as she knew him. Out of the steam, he evolved, ephemeral and alive.

She remembered...

Her father was the one who introduced her to photography. One day he needed someone to shoot pictures of his Golden Baby corn for an ad campaign. Instead of hiring a professional photographer, he asked her if she would help him. "Will you do it?" he asked her.

"I can try," she said. "But I don't know how the pictures will come out."

"It's basic stuff, isn't it? Focus and shoot."

How bad could the pictures turn out? After all, it was only corn she was shooting, and in broad daylight. So she borrowed Beatriz's camera and left with her father early one morning for the fields in Homestead.

The scenery rolled by, quite beautiful and serene. The furrows of the plowed earth flashed as they drove by. The migrant workers, her father told her, would soon be on their knees, their backs to the sun, picking the harvest. Farming was hard work. Back-breaking work.

They arrived by a large plot of planted corn. The plants grew like spears straight up. Her father peeled a bunch of ears and held them like gold in his hands. Like an offering to the gods.

"Take a picture of this," he told her.

She aimed and pressed the exposure button. Simple. She really didn't have to do much to the camera, not with its automatic focus and frame advance.

"These pictures," her father told her. "Will also be used in a conference I'm giving. I have to turn them into slides."

Her father posed some more, his boots dusty and muddy, firmly dug into the soft earth.

"Can you climb on top of the car?" he asked. "And take a bird's-eye-view shot of the fields?"

The car then was a Suburban, half-pickup, half-station wagon. She climbed on top of the vehicle and snapped some shots of the entire field, which, after they were developed, came out looking like a luscious wave of corn.

This was her first time out, and she did really well. She snapped a roll of twenty-four pictures. It was a sunny morning, and a slight breeze ruffled the leaves of the corn plants and whistled through the stalks. That was the morning her father told her why he did what he did, why he chose to work with corn.

On the way back to the house, he told her the story of corn, and how the civilizations in the Americas depended on it. It was their lifeblood. Any other crop could fail one year, but if corn didn't come through, many people would starve.

"That's why in a city like Mexico City," he told her, "if a wild corn plant grew in the middle of the *periférico*, the cars swerved around it."

To many civilizations, corn was holy. The Indians worshiped it, for they knew that without it a great catastrophe would occur.

Cristina recalled, too, that when her father paid for the ad campaign which appeared in all the trade magazines and during his conference, she got credit for having taken the pictures. The beauty of photography. What an idea it was: people and things forever preserved, forever still, even when in motion.

కింత

34
Secretary

One summer Beatriz worked for her father. She remembered all the frustrations of working for a man, who, without a doubt, was the only true perfectionist she'd ever known. Zacarías didn't understand time limitations.

Beatriz's days were spent typing and retyping, filing, organizing, and answering the telephone. She also edited and corrected misspelled words. She often translated the reports of one of her father's field employees, Juan Carlos Nieves. What language that man used, so flowery—his were Faulknerian-like reports, paragraph-long sentences.

And she often translated these reports while biting the inside of her lips. She chewed on her skin out of frustration until it tore and bled. But the work kept coming her way. Sometimes even in the middle of the night, especially if her father was under stress to meet a deadline.

These were the days when her father was getting contracts subsidized by the government. Washington showed no mercy; they wanted the job done fast and well.

She didn't know how her father did it; how he had the energy to focus and the nerves to work so hard.

By the end of the summer, Beatriz had lost fifteen pounds. She couldn't think of food; she didn't have the time nor the inclination. But she survived; she did it. She persevered because of her father. Oh, he rewarded her not only with money she didn't have the time to spend, but with love and affection.

She wanted the job because it offered her the chance to spend time with her father, who was abroad most of the time. Actually, for him it was an unusual summer spent in Miami.

He taught her about taking pride in one's work. "You must love what you do," he told her once. "If you don't, you cut back on your happiness. A person is measured, at least in this society, by what he or she does. How good you are is what's important."

She learned about professionalism. That job taught her many important lessons: discipline, patience, and endurance, too. Without these qualities, no person could be a professional. Zacarías, to her, became the embodiment of that word. Professional.

It seemed he was never satisfied, always strived for improvement.

That summer, yes, though she worked hard while her friends, cousins, and sisters tanned at the beach, she learned about work ethics. Now, she thought, her father left her with that much. She was a better person for it.

Her father would be remembered, she thought, not only by his family but also by all those who chose agricultural genetics as a field.

Yes, her father, through hard work, carved himself a place in the history of that field.

Zacarías, who was always more interested in work, his work, than in fame and fortune, though he told her once that those two elements followed if a person was the best in his or her field.

And this was the way Beatriz remembered her father.

৵৽৶

35
Super 8

Celia's uncle brought a camera from *Los Estados Unidos* one Christmas. It was the first of the Super 8 cameras with the easy-to-use chrome- and black-handled body. When the camera rolled, it made a soft whirring sound as the film moved. She was too young to understand the concept of film photography, but she was fascinated nevertheless. Her cousins were enthralled, too.

Her uncle always played director/cameraman; that was why he didn't appear in too many of the boxed rolls of film. (Her mother always talked about transferring the movies to video, and then giving everyone a copy.) So her uncle, while having a world of fun, shot roll after roll. He used to shoot the children eating, sleeping, playing leap frog, jump rope, and hopscotch.

There were the twenty rolls of their trip to Acapulco that same Christmas. The mountains blurred out of focus behind the bays where the waters sparkled among the shiny pebbles. The women stooped to wash clothes by the river banks. Naked children splashed water, floating on truck-tire inner tubes.

That Christmas was the only time she remembered her uncle being around all the time. He was there, but he was also studying for his Ph.D. at the University of Chapingo. Before, he was never home, away on his trips, or too busy to be seen. Her father was the same. Never home.

Her *tío* Zacarías was stern with them. When he was back in Lomas Verdes, the children couldn't play indoors. New rules about games were established. Her uncle often took them outside to play.

The yard in Lomas Verdes was an idyllic place to grow up. The houses were built so that the back of each house faced *areas comunes* or green community areas. Everyone knew everyone else. What mothers worried about in the big cities—kidnappers, cars, and crowds for example—didn't seem to trouble them in Lomas Verdes. Both her aunt and her mother allowed the children to play anywhere anytime. But Laura and Maura preferred to have their children indoors where they could keep an eye on them. When Zacarías played with them was an exception.

Everyone, meaning all the young couples who moved to the booming neighborhood Lomas Verdes development, had kids. All the mothers looked out for the safety of all the children.

That Christmas that Celia's uncle brought the camera, Samuel discovered the mound and they played King of the Hill. They rode Chacho's motorcycle, a little green machine with a real engine. You had to kick-start it and rev it up for a while.

Celia became Chacho's girlfriend that Christmas.

They rode the bike down the hill and loved it when they wiped out, even when they scratched their knees. It was painful though once their mothers washed their scratches with hydrogen peroxide and dabbed them with iodine.

Beatriz crashed the bike one time against a *pirul* tree because she saw their maternal grandmother coming up the path and the old woman scared Beatriz. She lost control and smashed head-on against the tree. She broke her right arm and split an eyebrow. The scar was still there.

That was how Zacarías found out about their playground.

Some mornings he went out with his camera and from behind the bushes took films of the children playing. They never spotted him.

That Super 8 camera brought out a different, more play-
ful, less serious man. Her uncle was fun to be around that
Christmas. He used to buy them all shaved ice from the ice
cream truck that came through their neighborhood. But once
the camera lost its charm, he gave it up, and reverted to his
old grumpy ways.

And trips.

He went on ever so many trips after that and only came
to town long enough to play the role of a disciplinarian.

This was Celia's version of her uncle. This was what she
chose to remember.

She never found out what happened to the camera, but
she knew her aunt kept all the films in a chest in the garage.
If they were not looked after soon and saved, time would take
its toll and all those wonderful days would be lost forever to
mold and mildew.

రీ~6

36

An Olympic Hopeful

Only Maura's brother-in-law knew the whole story and nothing less than the whole story about what she went through. Norberto and Laura only knew some of the crucial details of that morning, and the children had never been told.

A look of peace and eternal tranquility protected his face from the rictus of death. Zacarías lay still—her secret sharer. Only he could begin to understand part of the reasons why today she drank...he was there the morning of the tragic accident.

The incident ruined her career as an olympic hopeful. This was how it went: she was in Havana, training hard and long hours. Most mornings she woke up before dawn and practiced the javelin throw, which, even though she was to enter the women's Decathlon, was her strength.

If anything, she stood to win a medal for that one event. On the Cuban National Team, Zacarías ran the relay. He was fast then. *Look at him now.* Life was a joke! How could she think positively when she was surrounded by solemn women with their own grief and pain. She possessed her own.

That morning of the accident she was up and ready extra early. She carried the equipment to the field, and to her dismay found the field hidden by a thick blanket of fog. She decided not to waste her day. If she waited until the fog lifted, she'd lose valuable practice hours. She unpacked the javelin, laid it on the wet grass. She loved to rise early and smell the wet earth, that life-filled smell.

After she warmed up, she felt the tingle in her thighs and hamstrings. Her shoulders and arms were ready. The trick to the javelin throw was all in the release, the let-go snap. Poise was important too, and impulse, all parts of the body contributing in the motion of throwing.

She stood in position on one end of the field. Then it was a stadium field where the soccer team played and practiced. Not until the fog evaporated would she be able to see the marks of her reach after every throw. Maura stood back, held a steady grip on the javelin. Propelled by sure steps and gaining impulse, she reached the release point and hurled the javelin into the fog.

Maura thought she could hear it slice through the thick of it. She stopped to listen to the thud, the tip of the spear piercing and tearing into the grass at some distance, but instead she heard a horrible scream. At first she thought it was the cry of a sea gull. The stadium housed the nests of many sea gulls that flew in from the bay. They nested under the bleachers in the stands.

Then she heard a man scream.

The first scream had been brought out by pain, but the second was shock, and surprise. She ran into the fog to seek the origin of the scream.

Everything happened so quickly, so dreamlike, that for an instant she waited to be startled awake by the alarm clock.

She discovered a couple. A young man kneeling by a woman on the grass. Both were naked. The javelin had pierced the woman's skull and pinned her head back into the grass, the blow having killed her instantly.

Maura grew limp as she stood over the couple. She couldn't move or talk. The young man knelt by and tried in vain to resuscitate his girlfriend. It was then that Zacarías arrived. He had come out to run.

"Oh, my God, what am I going to do?" the young man cried.

Zacarías asked what they were doing on the field this early, though it was obvious what they had been doing. Zacarías wanted to know why here and not someplace else.

The young man had no shirt on and his pants were wrinkled like shed skin around his ankles. The woman's brassiere lay tangled in one of her arms.

"You are crazy," Zacarías told him.

Maura stood there looking down at the dead woman. Zacarías stood by her until the police and ambulance arrived. Some of the stadium keepers came. Zacarías and the young man vouched that it had in fact been a freak accident. The fog was still upon them when they carried away the body.

The bloodied javelin was removed and taken away. Zacarías held Maura when her legs gave underneath her weight. He kept telling her not to blame herself.

That was the morning she promised to stop being an athlete, and she did. By the next day the story had made the front page of the newspapers. Most headlines told of the bizarre incident. The dead woman had been a victim of chance. Maura had nothing to say. She promised to give up the sport immediately.

A day before the accident she had been an olympic hopeful, the following day a...there was no use, she could never bring back that young woman. She was gone and so were Maura's chances of continuing with the sport.

She wanted to attend the girl's funeral, but everyone in the family advised her not to. It would cause the girl's family too much grief. But she did pay the girl tribute by going to the cemetery weeks after the burial.

Maura went alone with flowers. She stood by the graveside and read the girl's name. Learned it. It was a name she was bound to remember for the rest of her life. Celia.

&∼⌒

37
What He Thought of Her

Not much.

Minuscule thoughts.

They really did rub each other the wrong way.

Perhaps he thought of her as the bitch who botched his son's life.

Oh, Sammy The Saint.

Okay. She never did try to make amends, but neither did her father-in-law.

Zacarías The Chauvinist.

He was wrong to think that his son, Sammy The Shmuck, was going to marry her, Gisell, and in her find a woman to cook, clean house, be the object of his desires, and bear him children.

Let us be serious, Oh Dead One!

Instead Sammy got whammy. Zippo. *Nada.* In his eyes, Dear Zacarías's, Sammy The Sailor (by engineering) got shafted. Ripped off. Robbed of a good life. Got a lemon in a raw deal.

Let the man rest, she thought. Besides, he was taking all his negative opinions with him.

Things like: "Son, you must put your foot down!" she actually walked in on father and son during such a conversation.

Zacarías, the macho pig.

Samuel The Snail had the *cojones* to tell her once that it wasn't his father's fault that he had inherited that *awful* (Sammy's favorite word, which he pronounces "offal") tradition.

Which tradition, Sammy?

Women as a beast of burden?

No way, Sam-o!

Not her.

Zacarías: "Don't let her stomp all over you, son."

Sure, she was stepping on him wearing stiletto heels.

"Don't let her push you around."

Push me back, Sam The Sham, with your green eggs (brown balls actually) and ham (salami: thick and stubby.)

Couldn't they be equals?

Zacarías, dear old daddy-in-law, Sammy might be free soon if their marriage didn't shape up.

You'd be happy to know it hadn't been a piece of cake, Gisell thought this, if she was allowed to be so unoriginal (that was what Zacarías called her once: unoriginal.)

The marriage was on the brink. She'd cut Sammy free, if that was what he wanted.

Okay. She was here to pay her respects. So stop thinking now.

Be polite.

Show a little respect for the dead.

৵৽৶

38

Gathered

Here they were, gathered, all the women (except for Cristina) of the Torres clan: Maura, Celia, Sofía, Beatriz, Gisell, Eleonor, and Laura, who didn't understand the reasons why Cristina chose to stay home. Her father's death must have shocked her into a sudden realization about life. Surely she must understand the concept which dictated that all life on the face of this earth must die.

The women stood by Laura, gave her comfort and hope. She and Maura had attended other funerals before—their parents' and Papi Torres's. But Laura chose Zacarías's to be different. Only family. Norberto and Samuel kept going out for *coladas*, Cuban espresso, and ham croquettes. They also brought guava and cream-cheese pastries, which people took turns eating outside the funeral home.

Gathered, they sat around the coffin, among the many sweet fragrant wreaths and bouquets, and they talked little. Small conversations about this and that. A few times she caught glimpses of her daughters crying.

A sad moment, but they must go on...in her mind she sang Zacarías the song she used to sing for him. "*Besos Salvajes.*" She used to sing it to him a cappella, when her voice came through soft and tender. It used to make her husband's eyes water with joy and exultation. She always sang the song in private, when they found themselves alone.

The song turned Zacarías on. Those nights they made love. Ah, most of her memories were pleasant. She and Zacarías met during Carnival in Havana. They had so much fun that night doing the conga, stuck in the middle of long conga lines, dancing to the beat and clamor of the *comparsas*...Maura had introduced them after she had that horrible accident.

Laura knew something had happened between her daughter Sofía and Ariel. She detected anguish in her daughter's eyes. They would talk when Sofía was ready. Though Sofía was far from being perfect, Laura guessed that Ariel must have done something despicable to her.

Rafael, Celia's boyfriend, arrived and gave Laura a kiss, then told her how sorry he was. He sat next to Celia and remained silent. She glanced at her sister eyeing her daughter and Rafael.

They made a good couple, Laura thought. If they were happy, what else mattered?

Lorenzo flew in from Mexico where he had managed to get emergency leave for two days from the Armada.

She looked at the men and realized that the Torres clan would sprout a new generation, with other family names, of course, but this thought made her happy. The lineage must continue.

Laura remembered her mother who once said that even in the largest of matriarchies, there must be men. Women must have their men, make room for them, but never take them too seriously.

Samuel and Gisell hadn't spoken to one another all night. This worried Laura.

Norberto, who once in a while stood by the coffin and lowered his head, tried his best to avoid his wife; he didn't want to deal with Maura, not if he could help it. Laura didn't blame either one. If Maura didn't mend her ways, she would lose him soon, for Norberto before his brother's death was going through middle-life crisis.

They must both work at getting their lives together again, and Norberto needed to be aware of his health. Laura thought he should go to the doctor for a thorough check up. Maura and Celia agreed.

Laura looked at Eleonor, so old and frail. Eleonor would die soon. Being the real matriarch of the family, she was worn out and disillusioned. Her eyesight was gone... Death had no prejudices. Eleonor, too, stood by the coffin and looked at her son.

The men slowly gathered and went outside to drink coffee, smoke, and talk. Juan Carlos joined them. As pallbearers they would carry Zacarías in and out of the chapel for the funeral mass. And they would carry him from the hearse to his grave, his final resting place tomorrow.

Tomorrow, Laura noted, would soon be upon them.

෬෧

Sexta

Burial

❧❧

39
Juan Carlos

During the mass, he recited the eulogy that he had spent the whole trip to Miami and most of the night composing for his friend and mentor, Zacarías Torres, Ph.d. Seed Genetics, a true professional, a great man. One of a kind. A family man, a good father, a man whose life had come to an end at the zenith of his career. Zacarías's achievements were numerous and notable. Many years of hard work and research left his mark in most Third World countries, from South Yemen to Punta del Fuego.

Zacarías took the time and had the dedication to help many people help themselves. No one understood the earth, its possibilities and qualities, the way Zacarías did. Indeed, Zacarías Torres would be missed from among those vast and endless fields where he labored and produced and harvested.

Parts of the eulogy would later appear in other forms in trade magazines and journals like the *American Seed Trade Association*, *Southern Seed Trade*, *Asociación Mexicana de Semilleros*, *Seedsmen*, *Seedsmen Digest*, and *Agricultural Digest*.

Juan Carlos, tall and proud to have this final chance to say farewell to a friend, teacher, and mentor, finished with the eulogy and asked for a minute of silence, and it was during this silence that the sound of pigeons flapping their wings against the stained-glass windows filled the church.

The moment of silent prayer was over and the ceremony continued.

∂∘∘

40

Norberto

He received the news at his hotel in Scott, Mississippi, home of Aaronson Pine & Land Corporation. **ZACARÍAS IS DEAD, RUSH HOME**. And he did, driving like a madman from Scott into Greenville, from where he booked the next flight out to Miami.

Now here he was, at his brother's burial, carrying his brother's remains on his shoulders. Twin brother, Zacarías. Norberto had been a pallbearer before, but he never imagined that he'd be carrying his brother's corpse. He and Zacarías had carried Papi Torres's remains. Norberto thought about life and death under the weight of his dead brother. It was like that song by Jose Alfredo Jiménez, "Caminos de Guanajuato." Life was worth nothing; nothing was life...but surprises, sometimes unpleasant ones.

This day at the cemetery rendered him speechless with so many bottled-up emotions. He felt dead in many ways. All it took was for one artery to clog up, get lined with layers upon layers of fat, and swoosh, you were a gonner.

He lamented his brother's passing, his brother who had lived the life of a good man. A hard worker, a family man. All in all he was always a good brother, though he and Norberto sometimes didn't see eye-to-eye on certain things.

When they were children, they meant the world to one another. They were the best of brothers and the best of friends. All those first years they slept in the same room, told each other wonderful ghost and adventure stories. Zacarías learned to read fast, so he read to Norberto when they both couldn't sleep.

Their father was one of the island's most prominent seedsmen back when they were children. The family had always been well off. Not rich, but on its own two feet. Strong and willing to break new ground. When they were children, they spent a lot of time with their father who often took them on cross-country trips. They loved the road and all the roadside attractions. It was the traveling that would later make them realize what they each wanted to do for the rest of their lives. Work the land and travel.

Looking back—it seemed to Norberto that they both had traveled a long way. But now his brother's venture had come to an end. To travel to new countries, to have the chance, was better than making a lot of money. A few years back, Zacarías visited South Yemen for the State Department. The report Zacarias wrote about the agricultural situation there and how it could be improved made him famous. It also helped the country by getting all the aid it desperately needed. Travel far, even if you don't make too much money—that was his brother's philosophy. The chances for someone to pay you to travel are, often in other people's lives, minimal or non-existent.

They traveled all the time, and Norberto wanted to believe that his brother was still doing so.

Yes, he looked up to his brother. Zacarías who had always done well in school. He studied, read, never received a grade lower than excellent. Norberto was so proud of him. Norberto was crushed when Zacarías decided to study at the University of Havana.

While away at the University of Havana, Zacarías met Laura through her sister, and a year later, after Carnival, they were married. They lived in the old section of town in an apartment over a *bodega*, a grocery store. Zacarías could only afford to pay the rent with the money his father sent him.

Norberto visited them during their vacations, especially when he was in Havana on business. It was during one of these visits that he met Maura, Laura's younger sister. No sooner had they met when he figured he'd be making more stops in the city.

It became a joke between them later—how two brothers could end up with two sisters. What were the odds of that happening?

Norberto and Maura saw each other more and more. He found excuses to travel to Havana, where he eventually relocated. Anything to be close to Maura and his brother.

Maura, during those days, had become involved with some people in the underground revolutionary movement. This was after she dropped all athletic activities. She often spoke of all the books she had read by Marx and Engels. She was a closet communist. When the revolution broke out in the Sierra Maestra, she contemplated joining it, but she didn't do it. Maybe, thanks to Norberto who had persuaded her not to, she made up her mind to stay in the city and let the revolution take its own direction.

After the triumph of the revolution, she joined the Ministry of the Interior. She became the Director of the National Council of Artists, which later, after 1965, disbanded and split into two warring factions.

Maura met all the influential writers and artists. He remembered she once told him she had had dinner with Jean Paul Sartre and his lady friend, Simone de Beauviour. Maura organized intellectual groups, often importing European and Asian writers and artists for national conferences. Her job made for some interesting times, which in fact would become Maura's happiest years.

Norberto and Maura didn't marry after the Torres's decided to leave the island. Zacarías took Laura to Mexico. Papi Torres and Eleonor moved to the States.

Maura wanted to stay, but she also loved Norberto. She made a deal with him: if she could stay one more year in her job, then she would marry him and leave the country. Norberto left for Mexico, and a year later found it impossible to return to the island. The government would not grant him a visa. He tried to get in, but the authorities wouldn't let him. Maura was also having trouble getting out. He married Maura by proxy. One of his friends stood for him at the wedding. Later in Mexico City, they would get married again. Zacarías was his best man, and Laura was Maura's maid of honor.

Such times together had made them inseparable, but here he was now carrying the body of his dead brother. Zacarías was no longer, and Norberto thought he'd be next. Ah, but starting today, he would take all the precautionary steps. In silence, he promised his brother he'd stop smoking and drinking. Starting today he'd take care of himself.

Norberto also promised to help Maura, for twenty-five years of marriage meant something. Yes sir, Norberto thought he could start a new life; all he had to do was stay alive.

৵৶

41
Samuel

He held on to the chrome-plated handles with a tight grip. The sharp, hard edge of the coffin bit into the flesh on his shoulder. While he carried the remains of his father, he thought the worse was yet to come. His life was a mess.

During the wake, he and his uncle Norberto talked about the company and how somebody had to take over. Norberto agreed to run it, and he needed his help. Samuel needed time to think. In the meantime he felt confused, worn down, and tired. But he knew he was not the kind to give up anything too easily. He was, as Gisell accusingly called him, a creature of habit. Maybe if Gisell wanted to stay in Miami, running the company with Norberto wouldn't be a bad idea, and he might be able to save his marriage.

Samuel needed time though. Enough to fly back to Maryland, pack, sell off the things they couldn't bring back or wouldn't want to, and resign. Having been given a security pass, he'd have to be debriefed, however long that process took.

Working on submarines had been an experience, but it was getting to him. All that time underwater. He was involved in a mission once that took him from Newport News, Virginia, to Punta del Fuego. The trip lasted thirty-two days. It was on a Trident, and they were testing all the sound equipment, radars and sonars. Then he thought those thirty-two days were to be the most difficult days of his life. But today, walking from the chapel to the grave under the harsh sun, was truly the most difficult. He understood how final death was.

At first the rest of the pallbearers had a hard time synchronizing their steps, but now, at a slow pace, they moved down the path in unison. Samuel caught himself sighing often, not getting enough air into his lungs.

Once they arrived at the grave, they gently placed the casket over the pulleys, a sling that would lower the coffin gradually to its final resting place.

After letting go, he stood back, feeling the pain of bruised flesh on his shoulder. The priest led them in prayer as the coffin began to go down. Into the ritual of burying the dead.

He lifted his head and saw his mother standing across the way. Behind her were Gisell and Norberto, weeping so hard his upper body shook. Behind them, the indifference of the sky.

He, Samuel, couldn't stand to see his mother cry. And she was crying behind the black veil. His eyes filled up, but he fought the tears back. He remembered what Zacarías told him at Papi Torres's funeral. "The death of your father is worse than your own."

Samuel stood still and succumbed to the pain and loss.

His father was the one who always told him that a man was born alone and must die alone. But he learned some important lessons a long time ago when he was twelve and his father sent him away to a boarding school in Switzerland. He was twelve, and had to leave Lomas Verdes, his family and friends. Zacarías thought the experience would be good for him, prepare him for life, but all he learned were the most basic rules of survival.

Up until the seventy-two days in the sub, the six months in Switzerland had been the worse days of his life. At school, he didn't get along with the other multi-nationality children. He hated them. The way they spoke and behaved. Of course, they hated him, too, but somehow he expected it. His accent, his dark looks, his curly hair, and his brute strength.

He tried to remember that time, but all the years of repressing those days had worked. He could not get in touch with the pain and hardships of those days. Well, except, the beating he received from the headmaster, a blond monster of a man who from the very beginning didn't like Samuel.

Samuel received the beating (and took it) because of a window he didn't break. Someone else came into his room and busted the window with a soccer ball. The headmaster found the deflated soccer ball under Samuel's bed. He got blamed even when he called upon his roommate to bear witness that the ball was not his.

That morning in the headmaster's office, he learned about hatred. Once the headmaster fell upon him with the paddle stick and he felt the first stings of wood on his flesh, he had to defend himself.

He reached for a letter opener/paper weight and stabbed the headmaster on the thigh, then he ran away. It seemed like he ran away all the way back to Lomas Verdes. Of course, his father was summoned and he came to the school and gave him the only beating he had ever given him. After that, he apologized to the school directors and headmaster and took him back home to Mexico City. He never again spoke to his father about that time.

Only he and his father knew about what had happened. Not even Gisell knew, and he didn't intend to ever tell her. Zacarías arranged it so that the incident would never appear on his son's records.

What he learned that day was something primal, something he knew he was capable of, though he didn't consider himself an irrational or violent person. Most of the time he was good-natured and pleasant

Samuel respected his father. His father lived for his career. Samuel used his to live. His father was not a family man; a family man, according to Samuel, was home more often. With his father it was the other way around. His father didn't know when to quit, and this is what got him at he end.

Samuel had other plans. He wanted a family, something other than work or being known for something. This his father mistook for lack of goals and aspirations.

But he didn't get to be an engineer without these two things, did he?

It was over; his father was buried and now everybody sought the coolness of their air-conditioned cars.

His father had returned to the earth...may God save his soul.

ॐ๛

42

Lorenzo

Lorenzo never really got to know Zacarías, but he flew in to pay his last respects. He helped carry the coffin out of the chapel and into the back of the hearse. He walked in silence behind the hearse as it made its way to the place of burial. Then once again they carried it to the grave and lowered it on to the pulley that would take the coffin down. Afterward, he returned to Beatriz's side. He was here to console her, offer her support and comfort, though not much had been said between them.

He would be with Beatriz for another thirty hours, and then he would have to return to Acapulco, from where he was to sail. Lorenzo was leaving early Tuesday morning.

Now, he stood still and silent and looked at his future bride's grieving face. She was beautiful. Her eyes, though strained by so many hours of tears, were still radiant. He remembered so many things about her. When they met, she was ten and he was twelve. His parents used to visit an uncle in Lomas Verdes, an uncle who lived in the same development the Torres' lived.

When they moved, she kept writing him letters. Once in a while, Zacarías would visit the house, while he was on business in Mexico, and Lorenzo would get to hear the family updates.

Zacarías brought pictures with him once, and he saw one of Beatriz. From then on he knew he wanted her. He wrote back and tried to convince her to come for a visit. She did a couple of times, and brought her youngest sister as a chaperon. Her sister Cristina and Lorenzo's brother started to date, but they were always arguing.

Lorenzo and Beatriz didn't become engaged until he entered the Armada. He knew he was going to be away at sea for eighteen months, training to become an officer on the Cuauhtémoc.

This, he figured, would give Beatriz enough time to think about what she wanted to do. She started to go to school at Florida International University, to become a pre-school teacher. She liked children, so she told him in her letters. She wrote more often than he did.

After the eighteen months away, he returned to shore for six months to study and prepare for the examinations.

By then, Beatriz had received an Associate's of Arts Degree, and wanted to finish and get her bachelor's. He agreed to wait. Anyway, he still had another two years with the Armada. At the end of those four years, although he planned to re-enlist because he owed the Armada another four years for paying for his education, he wanted to marry her.

Now, he was leaving on Tuesday, and he preferred to go back feeling secure, but he also thought he understood the time it takes to mourn. He let Beatriz know that. The wedding could be postponed for a while. Besides, on Tuesday he would return to the ship to spend another three months at sea.

ॐॐ

43

Rafael

The funeral procession began and ended the same way: four men carrying a coffin. Rafael held up the right rear, a heavy right rear. Not being the weakest or strongest, he wondered who was pulling most of the weight. No, he wouldn't say it to himself, but the thought rose to the surface anyway: dead weight.

They carried the coffin out of the chapel and into the hearse. This was his first funeral, so he didn't really know what to do.

The clouds moved in on the sun. This morning was beautiful, but it was beginning to change. Gray clouds brought the promise of rain. All around were the deep jades, emeralds, verdigris, *verdes*, yellow-greens, and browns of the trees and plants and flowers.

Everyone was dressed in black. All the women's faces seemed drawn from having stayed up all night. But worse of all were Laura and Maura—they seemed to have taken it the hardest, as hurt lingered on their faces.

Once the coffin was in the back of the hearse, the men returned to the side of their wives, girlfriends and friends, and walked down the path. They all followed the hearse as it moved at a snail's pace down the cobblestone way.

He remembered Zacarías as a good man, a family man. Descent and respectful. Rafael enjoyed being around the family and friends. Often when Zacarías told Laura to organize house parties and invite everyone, Rafael and Celia came to them with pleasure and had a great time.

Walking next to Celia, he felt inept and useless. Here they all were walking in a line, and he realized how little he could do to make Celia feel better. Celia, who walked shrouded in silence.

Hers was an everlasting expression of sadness and regret, of having understood something new about life and living, something she probably thought she'd never be privy to.

Cristina, he noticed, was not among them.

He reached over for Celia's hand (a dead wingless bird) and squeezed it as if to say, I understand.

Being five years older than she, he knew about the quick realizations of their own mortality. You must embrace it, he thought, and walk with it. Learn to live with the idea.

When he was eight, his grandmother died and nobody told him. His father kept from him the knowledge of death. She died and was gone forever. He had lived with the memories since.

Rafael noticed Maura gave them a side glance. They were not planning to get married. Why couldn't she understand? Their freedom was important, especially for Celia at this time. He wanted her to make sure she knew what she wanted first. Soon, she would quit work and embark on something new.

The beauty of knowing what you wanted to do with your life, he thought, was that once you knew, the rest was easy. It was a matter of enjoying the here and now. Yes, Maura, they intended to continue with their arrangement. With their understanding. To get married and do the ceremony thing would seem trite. Everything in their relationship had taken place naturally, at its own pace. Why fiddle with the restrictions of society? The rules? He'd always lived his life, or tried to, outside of these concepts.

No, they wouldn't be getting married, not yet. He'd always had good reasons for living on the outside. Society was no good; it could damage the artist's soul. Drain out of him all that mattered, all that was important to the heart.

Zacarías was buried, lowered into the arms of the earth. To rest in peace. The padre said his last words and the burial was over.

He and Celia would return to the routine and work of the living.

శ్రీం

Septima

Mourning

44

Once You're Gone
You Can't Come Back

Mortality baffled Cristina. It was such an abstract concept, but yet so real. Her father was buried now. The women in her family returned to the house. Her father had left this world, and she could never see him again. Her sense of beliefs failed her: why was it so easy to believe before? In the unseen forces of nature?

Cristina sat alone in her dark room and pondered all these circular questions. The ying-yangs of her reasoning. Sure, she became aware of the futility of thinking about her father when none of the questions she settled upon answering were going to bring him back.

Beyond the boundaries of the room, she heard the voices of the other women in her family. Their soft conversations, bits and pieces of them anyway.

Her mother and sisters were out there, beyond the walls... And she pondered how much different could her pain and sense of loss be from theirs.

They sat in the living room, for that was where the sounds came from, and bonded, using each other in their healing process.

And the process had begun...

She too would join in, when the time came. When she felt ready. In the meantime, she waited out her period of mourning in this room.

It was her way of coping; her family respected her wishes for solitude and introspection.

Cristina would understand soon enough, after she had pondered and questioned and meditated enough. She would emerge with a new perspective, even if she failed to answer all the essential questions about living and dying.

To her mind came those images captured in all the pictures she had taken on her way to Corpus Christi. The finality of death captured through the lens. The vicious cycles of nature.

It was in these images, she convinced herself, that God exists. God was nature; nature ruled over all life. It was in the concept of dying that the reasons for living existed.

Nature took its course no matter what happened.

Eventually, yes, she would emerge from this room with new insights, new visions, and things would make better sense.

She would see, for it was only a matter of time. And time was all she had.

ॐॐ

45
The Letter

Here they are, after the burial, all the women in Sofía's family, gathered in the house in Kendall. Her mother should be left alone, Sofía thought, so that she could rest. Norberto, Samuel, and Celia's boyfriend went to pick up something to eat. It seemed like they were taking forever. Everybody had voiced their hunger. Beatriz and Lorenzo were talking in the kitchen while Beatriz brewed a pot of espresso.

Cristina kept herself out of sight in her bedroom. She should be out here with the rest of them, sharing her thoughts. Sofía believed that with time her sister would understand, and with this new understanding she would leave her bedroom to continue with life as usual.

It did no good to hide, Sofía knew, you must confront the difficult moments in life head-on. With strength and dignity.

They were all sitting in the living room, a circle of sorts, when she saw a DHL courier van pull into the driveway. A man climbed out of the truck with a package. He approached the door and knocked.

She felt her heart skip a beat, for something told her the package had something to do with her.

Aunt Maura opened the door.

The courier said, "Package for Sofía Constantini."

She was right. Quickly, she went to the door, received the package, and signed where the man indicated. The courier left, got in back in the van, and disappeared around the corner.

Her aunt stood by her with a surprised look on her face. Well, she herself was not surprised. She even knew who the letter was from.

Constantini was Ariel's last name, so now everybody knew she had received a package from Ariel. She excused herself and went all the way down the hall to her mother's bedroom where she locked herself up. There she pulled open the big envelope and removed a letter.

That was all that she found in the package, and she began to read what the letter said:

Buenos Aires, Argentina
April 7, 19—

Sofía:

To safeguard against a possible "return to sender, address unknown"—which reminds me of the Elvis Presley tune—I am paying these people to deliver this letter.

I can imagine the man when he knocks and probably your mother or father, if he is home, opening the door. The man will say, "I have a letter for Mrs. Constantini." And your mother or father, having guessed it might be related to me, will respond, "No one here by that name."

I promised to get this letter into your hands somehow.

Now then, let me say that, if this is the way you want things, fine, you will have it your way. I understand how upset and determined you are. I truly understand, and I want to say so in this letter.

After this, I will grant you your wish—to never hear from me again. I will be out of your life forever. Pardon my melodramatic flair.

We go our separate ways.

I must ask you to at least hear me out, even if you believe this letter is nothing but a cheap excuse.

Everything has been my fault, I know. My neglect. But I also will not ask you for forgiveness. I intend to respect each and every one of your wishes. (Including letting Emilio keep the

Mercedes, even if he doesn't make enough money to repair it if it breaks down. But it will be as you wish.)

I am planning to sell this house and send you half of the money. I am also not doing it to be Mr. Nice Guy.

I have been a bastard and we both know it.

I am also glad that you have chosen to leave. Our love was over months before your decision. I know what you are probably thinking or calling me: coward! Yes, I agree. I was a coward not to confront you, and if I weren't one, I'd fly to Miami and tell you this face to face.

But I am a coward.

Listen, don't think you've wasted your time. I know you are going to go ahead and work on your degree. Something tells me you will, that those are your plans. Fine. You know I always encouraged you to do so. Enroll in one of those fine universities in the States and finish your career. The money from the sale of this house should pay for all of it.

One last thing and I will sign this letter.

You are probably wondering why I cheated on you. All I can say is that it was a stupid mistake, but the mistake taught me that I no longer loved you.

Sofía, you are free to do as you wish. The divorce papers are being drawn, and I think you will find the settlement more than fair. Sign them at your convenience when you receive them and return them to the law firm.

I wish you the best of luck with your new life.

Peace & Understanding,

Ariel

৯৵৩

46

Why She Can't Go Home Again

Gisell returned to her parents' house after the burial.

Her parents, who attended the ceremony, both took the day off.

This was her chance to break the news to them that she and Sammy were having problems, and that, if they separated, she might be coming back to stay with them for a while.

On the way back to the house, she rattled her brain for the right words, a combination of them to break the news to her non-talkative parents.

Her father, the accountant, had grown old. His hair had gotten grayer and more lines had attacked his face.

Like the lines of an Etcha-Sketch pad, a toy from her young girlhood.

She noticed that he was wearing a new pair of prescription glasses; their lenses were thicker. On his face were spots she hoped were not skin cancer.

Her mother, the secretary, still hadn't learned to apply make-up. Her lipstick smeared away from the lines of her lips. Too much rouge on her cheeks and the mascara was too dark a shade for her face.

Looking at her parents made Gisell very sad, and suddenly she felt lost in the leather back seat of her father's old Caddy.

They were getting old, and one day, they too would...

All the different ways in which she'd failed her parents became obvious to her.

She hadn't become the person they wanted her to be.

Oh, what a long list of grievances must they have if she were to ask them.

Where did she go wrong?

Where did they go wrong? they might ask.

They paid for her schooling in New Orleans, but nothing fruitful came of it and all their money was wasted.

Nothing she did in her childhood turned out right.

Her parents probably thought that the best thing that had happened to her was Samuel, the Torres's kid, who seemed to have a bright future and a lasting career as an engineer.

She searched for all the right words.

But came up empty by the time they arrived at the old house.

Nothing had changed.

Her parents kept the same flowers potted and planted around the house.

Half-wilted in the strong heat and light.

The same color on the walls.

The stains from the sprinklers on the cinder-block fence extended in large arcs.

This was where she grew up.

Not much had changed indeed.

Inside, her parents kept the place simple and drab.

Boring.

No vivid or lively colors here.

Same ornaments and pictures on the walls.

Clean on the surface, but dusty, she knew, in the unseen places. Dusty.

It was as if time had been encapsulated here, trapped.

Everything had gone unchanged, and that included her parents' life.

The same smells she was once familiar with linger in the air: garlic, pine fresh scents, dead roses...

When they had Sputnik, the Pomeranian, the house smelled of dog food and dog shit. That Pomeranian was a real shitter.

That was all he did, eat, sleep, and shit. Oh, and bark at everyone.

Samuel, when they were dating, came to this house often, especially if her parents were away visiting friends or on vacation.

He came over all the time, when his or her hormones kicked in, which was all the time.

They fucked all over the house.

Sputnik and Sammy didn't get along, so they had to keep the dog locked up in the hall closet and listened to him whimper and bark and scratch behind the door.

Eventually, Sammy and Sputnik had a confrontation.

It was during one of those nights she took great care and stealth to sneak Sammy into her room through the bedroom window.

When this happened, Sputnik would sniff under the crack of her bedroom door and detect Samuel's smell.

Sammy often smelled of strong cologne, or was it the smell of his hormones?

The musk of their lovemaking?

Sputnik would bark and bark and bark.

Suddenly, Sammy opened the door and grabbed the dog, which bit Sammy's hand, and Sammy threw him into a pillow case, tied the mouth of the case with a shoe string, and hung the dog out of the window until they were through with their lovemaking.

And what scenes those nights were...

శ్రీం

Her mother and father changed into more comfortable clothes.

Gisell kicked off her shoes.

Her mother went about the kitchen asking them what she should prepare for lunch.

"You are staying for lunch, yes?" her mother asked.

"Sure. What are you thinking of making?"

"Nothing fancy. I'm looking to see."

Estoy viendo. She remembered this same phrase her mother used throughout all the years.

I am seeing.

Now that her father had walked out onto the patio, Gisell relaxed.

She was always closer to her mother, especially regarding her private matters.

"Samuel and I are not doing too well," she finally decided to tell her mother.

"Oh," her mother said, not looking at her but continuing to open cupboards and the refrigerator in search of condiments and things.

Her mother removed a whole chicken from the freezer, took the plastic wrapper off, and left it to thaw in the sink. She would have to put it in the microwave to defrost, if she wanted it done faster.

"I want to move down here," she said. "Back to Miami."

Her mother chopped green peppers and onions.

"I don't know what effect his father's death will have on Sammy."

"Somebody has to run the company."

"Norberto'll probably do it."

The chopping continued with the knife hitting the cutting board, the thuck-thuck-thuck drowned out the silence between them.

All through the years there had been so much silence between them, Gisell thought.

"I think it'll do us both good to separate for a while," she added.

Her mother stopped chopping. "What for?"

"To see."

"See what?"

"What happens."

"What do you think will happen?"

"I don't know."

"Don't act in haste," her mother told her, and absent-mindedly pointed the knife at her. "Think about this. That's what I recommend you do before you make a mistake."

"That's the only way I know how—"

"You might be sorry later."

"What are you saying?" she asked her mother.

"I don't know, I mean—" she began, and stopped to scoop the julienne-cut peppers onto a plate. "It's your life. You do what you must. If that's what will make you happy, do it."

"That's what I mean," she continued. "I don't know if being away from him will make me happy."

"Personally, I don't think this is a good time for you to leave Samuel. He's going through tough times, I know."

"I was thinking of staying here for a while."

Her mother looked up at her in disbelief. "I don't think your father—"

"What are you saying, mother?" she said, feeling the surface of the barstool she'd been sitting on get harder and more uncomfortable.

Gisell stood and leaned against the counter.

"Sure, you can stay here, but only for a while."

Only for a while. How long was that?

"I don't think it would be good for your father and I to start up the old friction."

This business about friction was news to her.

"Friction?"

"What do you think, dear? That raising you was easy? Look, if you moved back in, your father and I would start arguing again. If I worry, he'll get upset. If you start going out late at night, he'll—"

"Mother, I'm an adult. And I expect to be treated like one."

"Remember, this is *his* house and you must abide by *his* rules!"

"A little respect."

She wasn't listening.

"Are you willing to do as he wants you to do, if you come back?"

"Mutual respect, and I don't see what that has to do with—"

"Everything. You come back, and the trouble starts. He'll tell you he doesn't want you going out and coming back late, and you won't respect his wishes."

"I can't believe you."

"Believe me, I know what I'm talking about."

"So what you are implying is that I better think twice about coming back."

"Yes, that's precisely what I recommend."

"Wonderful."

"If you still want to leave Samuel and want freedom to come and go as you please, then I suggest that you rent an apartment."

Gisell found it difficult to restrain her anger and dismay.

"Thanks for the words of wisdom."

"You jump to conclusions too fast," her mother said.

Gisell moved back away from the counter in order not to get the damned spray from the onions her mother was cutting in her eyes.

Her mother continued with what ended up turning into a sermon: "I want to help you; you are my daughter. But as you claim, you are an adult now and I'm treating you as one. I am talking to you as a woman who also happens to be your mother. Woman to woman, right? When you were growing up, I did my best for you. So did your father, but we are too old to start that up all over again...

"It'll destroy our marriage, and I'm too old to lose your father. He's too old to lose me."

"If that's the way you feel."

"I say you don't leave your husband. If you feel you've made a mistake, stand by it and work at correcting it. In life you must change."

Spare me, she said to herself.

Her mother got a frying pan on the stove, turned on the heat, and sautéd the onions and peppers in butter.

"So if you want lunch," she said, wiping her brow, "I'm working on it."

Her mother, Gisell understood now, was turning her away.

Fine.

She'd learn to live with it as she'd learned to live with so many other things.

෫෧

47
Worn & Tired

Laura sat among her family: children, sister, and the men. Out of politeness, she continued to listen to all their conversations. Though she was worn and tired, she stayed put. The last four days had taken their toll on her body and mind, and she couldn't help but feel hollow. Her mother-in-law had not said much. Maybe she was famished like the rest of them.

Norberto, Samuel, and Celia's boyfriend returned with Chinese food wrapped in brown paper bags. Special fried rice and plenty of spicy honey chicken. The instant the food arrived, she and Maura set out the dishes and silverware on the dining room table.

Maybe, Laura thought, after they ate, everybody would allow her a bit of peace and quiet. She wanted to be alone for a change.

As quickly as the food was unwrapped and placed on the table, everybody gathered around and began to serve themselves. Everybody swarmed around the table without saying much. The rattle of the silverware hitting china filled the silence. One by one, they served themselves and returned to their seats by the coffee table in the living room, where all the paintings of mothers with children hung. It was a motif Zacarías started with a painting he brought her from Nicaragua for Mothers' Day. Throughout his travels in Latin America, he often commissioned local artists and sculptors to paint or sculpt a mother and child.

Most of these hanging on the wall were of Indian women with their children. Peasant women with dark skin and deep humility engraved on their faces. They were content with the products of the earth and with their children.

Her family. She looked at them as they ate. They sat among these paintings and sculptures. She felt her pride swell up within her, tugging at her being. They were a family of strong women—determined to survive no matter what circumstances.

Here they were. They ate in silence. They ate and avoided eye contact, too intent on eating, especially her sister and Norberto. She had often wondered how long their marriage would last. It suddenly dawned on her while looking around at her family that she was a widow now.

Una viuda. A widow. She filled with a great sadness and stopped eating.

Maura noticed her sister had stopped chewing.

Laura nodded, looking at her family looking at her. After a brief pause, she said, "I thank you all for being here."

Everything happened so fast, and all of it was now catching up with her. She didn't want to feel sorry for herself.

"What you need," Maura added, "is a lot of rest."

"What I need," she answered, "is to stop thinking."

Then, as if to put into practice what she had suggested, she stood up and walked over to Cristina's room.

She tapped on the door. No response.

She said, "Cristina, there's food out here. If you get hungry..."

"I'm not hungry," came her voice from behind the door. "Thanks."

"Okay, *corazón.*"

Laura returned to the living room to join her family.

Earlier, when Sofía received the package, she had disappeared into one of the rooms, but now she was back among them.

After she was done eating, Sofía put away her plate and silverware and returned to announce that she and Ariel were getting divorced.

She didn't say it too loud.

Nobody said anything. What could they tell her? That she was doing the right thing? If she wasn't happy, she was definitely doing the right thing. For she was still young enough to start again.

"What are you going to do now?" Norberto asked her.

"I'm going back to school."

"Good for you," Maura said, and smiled.

As far as Laura knew, her sister Maura hadn't had a drop of alcohol. At least she hadn't seen her pouring any.

Maybe Zacarías's death would bring about some good changes in her, Laura thought.

"I'm exhausted," Eleonor said.

"You want to lay down?" Laura asked her mother-in-law.

"I'd like to go home when someone can take me."

"I can take you, mother," Norberto told her.

"Finish eating first," she said.

"You are welcome to stay," Maura told her. "Or you can go to the house."

The house, of course, was Casa Maura.

"I might as well go home, to my house."

ॐॐ

After everyone was done eating, Sofía, Beatriz, and Celia did the dishes and in no time they had everything cleaned and the dining room table spotless. Those three worked fast and hard, Laura thought of her daughters and her niece.

Now Beatriz was going to brew some Bustelo coffee, which Laura didn't plan to drink. Otherwise, she wouldn't be able to take a nap.

The phone rang. It was Gisell calling for Sammy to go pick her up at her parents'.

Juan Carlos asked Sammy to drop him off at the airport. He needed to return to the fields in Latinia and finish what Zacarías had begun four days ago.

"Take care of yourself," Juan Carlos told Laura.

"Thank you for all your help."

"I'll keep in touch."

"Please do."

"And you let me know if there is anything I can do for you," he added, and they hugged.

"Have a good trip back."

He and Samuel left. Laura watched them go down the street and turn the corner.

Beatriz finished the coffee and brought it out to everybody in the living room. Maura and Norberto, Celia, Rafael, Sofía, and Lorenzo drank. Then Beatriz collected all the little *tacitas* and returned them to the sink in the kitchen. She and Lorenzo left for the patio where they sat and talked and smoked by the pool.

Cristina remained in her room.

Rafael left because he had to work in the gallery. His opening night was approaching. Celia, who asked her parents if they could drop her off at the apartment later, stayed, but she didn't want to get home too late; she was going to work tomorrow.

Celia sneezed. "This," she said, "tells me I don't want to go back to work."

Norberto took Eleonor home.

Sofía excused herself and returned to one of the bedrooms. Gradually everyone left, and now both sisters found themselves alone. This became the perfect chance for them to talk. But they were both worn and tired. They found themselves speechless, as if all that needed to be said had been said.

48
Waiting Rooms

Eleonor's son, the only one left her, drove her back to the house. Back to her routines. Back to remembrance and pain and sleepless nights. Sleepless because of the *culebrilla*, which was some strange disease she had in her legs. They called it *culebrilla* (the little snake) because she got these sensations up and down her leg, as if something were crawling under her skin.

Norberto was quiet. She imagined he was thinking about his own death. When that day came, she would not be in this world.

"They told me," she began as he pulled into the driveway of the house where Papi Torres used to park his Oldsmobile, "too late. I'm always the last to find out about anything."

La ultima en enterarse de todo, she was.

"They wanted to spare you, *mamá*," Norberto told her.

"Of my own son's death?"

"Heartache. To spare you of the heartache."

"I already have that. Have had enough. I'm immune to it by now, don't you think? I can take it."

"You are stronger than any of us."

"Don't be ridiculous," she said.

"It's true. You are healthy and strong."

"I'm falling apart." She truly was. Slowly, too, bit by bit. More so in recent years. In all these years (eighty-seven, to be exact), the pains and aches had taken her by storm.

They sat in the car. Underneath her she felt the hum of the engine idling.

"I will be dying soon, too," she told her son.

He looked at her in disbelief, as if she were telling him something he didn't know, or didn't want to believe.

"Nonsense," he responded.

"Next thing you will tell me is that I have more years left."

"Oh, but you do, mamá."

"Very well then," she said, and paused to clear her voice. "If that's the case, then I make you the following proposition."

She paused again.

The housekeeper/grannysitter, as she always called her, opened the door and looked out, waiting for them to get out of the car. They stayed put until Eleonor was done talking.

"You want to go inside?" Eleonor asked.

"No, thank you," he said. "I must run."

She gestured for the housekeeper to wait. She'd be in the house shortly, when she was good and ready.

"What's the proposition?" he asked.

Eleonor hooked him. "I want to be visited," she said. "I want to see my grandchildren more often."

"Don't they visit?"

"You call seeing them at family gatherings a visit?"

"No."

"I also want you to come by at least once a week," she said.

"I will if I stay in town."

"I'm serious."

"I wouldn't think otherwise," he said.

"You come visit."

"The company needs someone to look after it."

"I don't care about the company," she said sternly. "I care about seeing you."

"You will," he added. "More often."

"My days are so long," she said.

"I feel like twenty-four hours a day is not enough."

"Learn to pace yourself," she told him.

"I forget sometimes."

"Don't go so fast."

"I will tell everybody to come see you," he said, and smiled faintly.

"I don't want it to be a burden on anybody," she said.

"Don't think that."

"I can't help it," she continued. "Especially living in there." She pointed to the house. "So big. All those empty rooms. All the memories, but I'm tired of the silence."

"I'll visit you," he said. "You have my word."

"Good," she said.

He reached over and unclasped her seat belt. Then he came around the front of the car, opened her door, and helped her out. He waved the housekeeper over to give his mother a hand getting back to the house. Eleonor reached over and leaned into him to kiss him goodbye.

"Goodbye, mother," he said. "Take care, and call if you need anything."

She stood there next to the housekeeper who was holding her elbow and waved goodbye to her son.

When Norberto left, it was back to the house. Back to all the empty rooms, all that silence where her death awaited, she thought.

❧⟡

49

Tomorrow's Departure

Beatriz and Lorenzo sat by the pool and didn't say much to each other. She looked at a bee struggle on the surface of the water. It tried to climb onto the tiles by the edge, to survive, to dry its wings, and continue its flight to the next flower.

The temperature was hot, but not too humid. The clouds that had gathered earlier while they were at the cemetery had dissipated. Once again the sky was clear and blue and bright, like so many other early afternoons.

They were sitting among her father's plants and flowers, which somebody had to water.

The breeze swept the bee away from the tiled edge of the pool to the center.

"Maybe I should resign from the Armada," he said, "and open our own Chinese restaurant."

He laughed.

She didn't think this was funny. "Be serious."

"I am."

They fell silent again, and again he spoke first: "How long do you need?"

"For what?"

"To decide."

"What we should do?"

"We know what we have to do."

"Yes."

"Let me know."

"I'll let you know."

"You don't know what it is like," he said, and turned to her. "To have to wait. To be at sea and have to wait."

"I understand," she said. "But I can't give you an answer now."

"Nothing has changed between us, has it?"

"I don't think so. No."

"You sound unsure."

"Nothing has changed."

"You still want to marry me?"

"Yes."

He reached for her hand. "I want us to be together as soon as possible. Stay together for good. I want you with me all the time."

"I feel the same," Beatriz told him, "but I need a little time. I want to stay close to my mother. She needs me now."

He interrupted. "You are not her only daughter."

"I know, but its good now that we are all here to give her support."

The bee wasn't going to make it.

"I fear they'll talk you out of it," he said with a crackle of urgency in his voice. "I don't know, Sofía's not at the best moment of her life. Samuel and Gisell, well, you can see it on their faces."

Beatriz laughed softly. "What makes you think such a silly thing. I have a mind of my own. We *will* get married."

"Soon?"

"Yes, soon."

"I leave on the ship Tuesday."

"You've told me. That's tomorrow."

He kissed her.

"Keep yourself busy."

"On a destroyer?"

"Write me. Write me lots of letters."

"I hate to write letters," he said. "I want you next to me. Closer than paper and ink."

She couldn't stand to see the bee struggling, so she stood up, grabbed the pool net from the hooks on the screen posts and swept it along, pushing the bee, scooping it and dropping it on the pebbled surface of the walkway.

"There," she said, and put the net and poll back on the hooks.

"What is it?"

"A bee. It was drowning."

"Maybe when it dries its wings, it'll fly over here and sting you." He smiled. "To show you its gratitude."

"Should we go inside?" she asked.

"It's nice out here."

"Okay, we'll stay out here."

"Maybe there'll be other insects that will need your help."

They both laughed.

"I like talking to you."

"We really haven't been saying much," she said.

"That's because I don't know what you are thinking."

"I'm not thinking about much."

"I know it's been a draining experience," he said. "When my grandfather died, I felt hollow for days. I couldn't eat."

"I have no trouble accepting it," she added. "But I can't understand it when it happens so quickly, by surprise like that."

"Your father was too young to go any other way."

She thought about this.

Her aunt Maura opened the kitchen window to ask them if they'd like something to drink. They both asked her for Cokes. In no time, Maura brought them a glass of Coke each and placed them on the table. They thanked her and she returned inside.

"Norberto told me he and Samuel plan to run the company," he said.

"That's what they say," Beatriz said. "But Sammy has Gisell to worry about."

"He says she want to stay here now."

"She changes her mind so often, nobody knows what she wants. Not even her."

"I haven't seen them together since they got here."

"I've stopped thinking about it," she said.

"Anyway," he continued, "I think it's good that Norberto'll stay in town."

"Good for Maura."

The Coke glasses were wet and they left circles on the plastic patio table. The crushed ice melted quickly in the heat.

"When I get back to Acapulco," he said. "I'll try to call you."

"I'll be here waiting."

"Will you have a better idea by then?" he asked. "About resuming our plans?"

"I didn't think otherwise," she said. "Leave it alone. You know what my answer is."

He smiled. "I think so."

"Good."

"When I get on the plane tonight and sail tomorrow, I can leave with peace of mind."

They continued to sit by the pool in the heat and drank their Cokes, and she looked at the surface of the pool for any more drowning insects.

⊰•⊱

50
Trio

Before her father returned from taking Eleonor home, Celia told her boyfriend that she was going to stick around for a while, that maybe the opportunity to talk with her mother would arise. Rafael said goodbye to her aunt, mother, and cousin Sofía, and left for the gallery, since he intended to get some more work for the opening night done. Celia's parents would drop her off on their way back to Coral Gables.

The only man in the house now was Lorenzo, and he was out by the pool with Beatriz.

Her aunt, mother, cousin Sofía, and herself remained gathered about the living room coffee table. Sofía was talking about her immediate plans. She intended to find a job, part-time, and enroll at Florida International University. Ariel, she said, was behind her. Out of her life for good.

Good for Sofía.

Neither her mother nor aunt interrupted her cousin. They let her talk, get things off her chest, so to speak. They sat and listened to her.

Sofía disclosed the story about Ariel's infidelity. It turned into a long story of deceit and lies, which ended with her in Buenos Aires packing up and making her mind up to leave. Good for her, Celia thought, she had done the right thing.

There was no reason why a woman should feel trapped into a relationship, even a marriage. If it wasn't good, then leave—it was your right.

The phone rang. Celia hurried to the kitchen where the nearest phone was and picked up the receiver.

"Celia," the voice said. "This is Grace."

"Hello, Grace."

"Sorry about your uncle," she said. "Tell your aunt I will stop by to see her when I get back."

"Where are you now?"

"I'm still in Corpus Christi."

"This is costing you then," Celia told her.

"It's okay," she said. Then, "Is Cristina there? I've got something I want to tell her."

"Hold on," Celia said, and placed the receiver on the kitchen table. She went to Cristina's room and knocked. She said, "Cristi, it's Grace."

Silence.

She waited for a reply.

"Tell her I'll talk to her later," Cristina's voice came from behind her locked door.

Celia returned to the phone and gave Grace the message.

"She's taking it pretty hard, eh?" Grace said.

"She'll snap out of it."

"I don't blame her," Grace said.

Grace's father, Celia knew, abandoned the family when Grace was still a baby. Her mother raised her, a single parent, and Grace still lived at home with her.

"You want me to tell her something?"

"No, thanks, I'll call her back."

"When are you coming back?"

"Soon."

"Well, take care."

"Bye."

They hung up and Celia returned to the living room, where the conversation had changed to Samuel and Gisell and how things didn't look right between them.

Her mother told them about Samuel saying the very same thing the night he arrived in Miami with Gisell.

"If they break up," Laura said, "fine. Samuel knows what he needs to do."

"It doesn't make sense," Sofía said, and stood up to go to the kitchen. Then, "More drinks?"

They all said no.

Maura was not drinking, or at least they hadn't seen her make herself a drink. They all wondered how steady she was.

Celia's father returned and told everybody what Eleonor, his mother, had complained about.

"It's true," Laura admitted. "We've abandoned her. We should see her more often."

"She's hurt she was the last one to find out about Zacarías."

"It's no one's fault. That's the way it happened," added Maura.

"We have to spend more time with her," he said. "And that goes for her grandchildren, too." He looked at Celia and Sofía who returned from the kitchen eating ice cream bars.

"With school, dad," Celia said, "I'm always too busy."

"Once in a while," he told her. "Won't hurt."

"Okay." She'd visit her grandmother once in a while.

"Will you guys take me home?" she asked her parents. "When you are ready. I've got to prepare lesson plans for tomorrow."

"Let's go," her father said, and stood up. "I'm ready now. I also want to start early tomorrow morning. I have to call Mississippi and tell them the deal is off."

Her mother grabbed her purse and was ready to go. They said goodbye to her aunt and cousin. Celia said goodbye to Beatriz and Lorenzo through the kitchen window. They waved back.

She and her parents left the house in Kendall.

It had been a tough day. Week. A long time it seemed. For all of them.

Now it's the three of them, and Celia wished somebody would start talking so they could open up and talk, communicate, say the things that had been bottled up for so long between them: her mother's drinking, her father never being home, and her moving out on her own. She had broken the triangle, but she had to.

Would someone speak, Celia thought, for she couldn't bring herself to do it. The words must come from them; they were her parents. She is their daughter.

But it didn't happen.

കൈ

51

Steadfast Sammy & The Steady

Sammy picked her up in front of the house.

Her parents' old house; hers no longer.

Sammy The Steady, The Punctual, The Saviour, came to her rescue.

Noticing the deep dark blue half-moons under his eyes, she climbed in and buckled up next to him.

Her parents closed the front door on her before she got to wave goodbye.

She felt like shit, but she refused to show it.

"Where shall we go?" he asked.

Sammy The Silent spoke out.

"Wherever you want," she said.

After the conversation with her mother, she didn't feel like arguing. Minuscule things wouldn't get to her anymore. She wanted to be a new person.

"Sammy," she began, and stopped.

He listened.

"I'm really sorry about all this."

"So am I."

"I've treated you like shit."

"It's the other way around," he said. "I haven't been paying attention to you."

"How could you? When your father—"

"It's my fault."

Sammy The Martyr blamed himself.

She would not let him take the blame this time.

"What are we going to do?" she asked.

"I don't know," he added. "What do you think?"

"I think you need me, and I need you. As corny as it all
may sound."

"I don't think it sounds corny at all."

"But we need help."

"What kind of help?"

"Counseling."

"There's too much going on—"

"I don't mean right now."

"Later, yeah okay. Later on is fine."

He drove on and on and on.

"I believe it'll do us a lot of good."

"I think so, too."

He was not taking her to his parents. He turned at a light
and got on the expressway.

They headed east toward the downtown.

"We need to talk, yes," she said.

"About a lot of things," he agreed.

The view was pretty so distant out of the car windows.

"We should drive up US 1, up the coast and see the
beach," she said.

"That's fine," he said. "Let's talk while we drive."

On the way he told her what she wanted to hear:

They would move down from Maryland, that cold and
indifferent place.

They would sell the town house.

They would get rid of the stuff they didn't want or need.

They would start again here in the Magic City.

They would spend more time together, now that he
planned to start work with his uncle.

Spend more time together, less time at work.

She would get a job and keep herself busy.

They would save up for a house; in the meantime they
could rent an apartment.

She liked the sound of what he was saying.

Sammy The Steadfast, Sammy The Steady. He sounded
motivated and determined.

It was enough to make her want to catch on.

If they stayed together, they would strengthen the foundations of their marriage.

If they broke up, they lost everything, including themselves.

So true. So true.

And the stones and pillars of their foundation needed to be strengthened, she knew.

They would start anew.

Once they got settled, they could start their joint therapy as a couple who were willing, who had reached the crucial point, a new level of maturity, and who welcomed constructive criticism about themselves and the way they were living.

Yes, outside help to help them on the inside.

Anything that helped them stay together.

Sammy headed up the coast, hands on the wheel, eyes on the road, almost a smile on his lips.

They were thinking.

Talking.

Communicating at last.

His feelings, hers. She sat back and listened to his ideas.

Yes, she liked very much what she heard.

Steady, driving steady.

The sound of his words reached her like a lullaby, and, for the time being, she believed she could tap into a new well of inner peace and tranquility.

She truly believed they could scratch off the stuff of the past and light up a new present and future. She believed all this and more.

52

Second Place

Cristina emerged from her room at last, resigned to the fact that her father had died. She left the room in search of her mother. Cristina wished to say that she was all right now. She had made it. Also, she was very hungry. She walked through the house like a somnambulist and it all seemed so new to her, strange and unfamiliar.

Her mother was asleep in the master bedroom. She's on her own corner of the bed, looking so small in so much space.

She decided not to disturb her. Let her sleep. God knew they all needed it, her mother most of all.

Where was everybody else? Her sisters must have gone out.

In the living room, she stopped to look through the sliding glass door at her father's garden. She would take it upon herself to water the plants as often as possible. She leaned against the glass and stared out, as if transfixed.

The phone rang.

Cristina snapped out of her pensive state and hurried to the kitchen to answer. She didn't want it to wake up her mother. On mid-ring, she answered.

"Cristina?" She recognized Grace's voice. "Is that you?"

"Yes, Grace."

"Did Celia tell you I had called."

"Yes, she did."

"I feel awful about your father," Grace said, and after a pause she went on to ask, "How are you doing?"

"Okay. Better," Cristina answered.

"Good," said her friend.

She could hear the sound of traffic rushing by in the background.

"Where are you?"

"Back on the road," Grace informed her. "Nubi and I are driving back. I didn't think I was going to get you on the phone, but I decided to keep trying."

"What happened?"

"Are you ready?" she asked. "For the good news?"

"I'm ready."

"You won second place in the contest."

Cristina sighed. She had expected to win the grand prize, the trip to Italy for the summer, but second place, she figured, was better than nothing.

"Cristina?"

"I'm still here."

"Aren't you excited?"

"What did I win?" she asked.

"New equipment and a year's supply of Kodak paper."

"That's great," she said, picking up her enthusiasm. "You guys must have done a hell of a job mounting and framing the pictures."

"It wasn't that bad. Those pictures are good."

"You guys can pick and choose the ones you want."

"You mean it?"

"You bet," she said. "When are you guys getting here?"

"In a couple of days," Grace said. "We plan to stay over in Pensacola for the night."

"I see."

"Then we'll drive straight to Miami. I'll stop by as soon as we get in."

"What did the judges say of my work?"

"They wouldn't give us that information. You have to write them for it."

"Okay."

"Hey, listen," said her friend. "I gotta go. Nubi's waiting."

"See you soon."

"*Adiós.*"

They hung up.

Slowly, the excitement started to build within her. She won second place. She wondered what kind of equipment she'd won. A camera? Lenses? Lab chemicals? Maybe all? It was a respectable contest.

Strange, she thought, how in the midst of something bad happening, good things can happen too. Perhaps her father's spirit was with her, to guide and protect her from now on. She liked to believe that. The thought raised goose pimples all over her skin thinking about it.

At least it was wonderful and reassuring to think so.

❧∝

53

Self Help

Maura and Norberto dropped their daughter off in the apartment Celia shared with Rafael. Then they drove back to Casa Maura in silence. They drove in the long tunnels made by the branches of the banyan trees. Maura was thinking of nothing in particular, and everything in general. To begin with a clean slate, she would return to the house and give it a good cleaning. Clean the kitchen, scrub the floors with Pine Sol, and bury the stench of spilt liquor.

She would fix what needed fixing; organize the cupboards; empty the refrigerator. Throw away the junk that cluttered her living space. She was going to get busy and stay busy. No slack time to think about anything. As soon as she was done with the house, she was going to find herself a job. Yes, work. That would help her take care of most of her day. She told Norberto she was going to get a job.

Norberto said that maybe she could help him with the books at the office.

Once home, Norberto picked up all the unread newspapers on the lawn. She opened the door and entered the house. Immediately, she kicked off her shoes. Her feet still hurt from all the cuts. She found a pair of old slippers in a hall closet and put them on. She was determined to help herself. She'd never needed anybody to help her recover from her drinking binges. She always stopped them.

Yes, all she needed was determination and will power and she'd do it. No more drinking. Everybody deserved a new beginning, and this was hers. A new chance. No Alcoholics Anonymous or therapy groups for her. Not when she could do it on her own, like she'd done several times before. She remembered how quickly she recouped after she had the accident.

If she did it on her own, then she could doubly relish her triumphs. This was it, time to begin again. Get going with her life, because tough or not, pleasant or unpleasant, sad or happy, difficult or easy, she was going to live through it. The time had come to clean up her life and move forward. Forward to new and interesting possibilities.

&oe&

Octava

Last Words

54

Lesson Plans

Celia's parents dropped her off. Now she was back to her apartment. Alone again. Entering, she heard Jane shouting at her daughter. Not much had changed. She returned to the fish and the cats. Wasabi and Sato greeted her in the kitchen. They jumped on top of the kitchen counter and purred to be petted, and she did, then they meowed to let her know they were hungry.

Rafael had not returned from the gallery. It was good to be alone. Being around the family for so many hours drained her. She still felt numb about her uncle's death. Her uncle's remains rested in peace in a nice place. Shadyhill Cemetery looked beautiful, with all the huge banyan trees and the vast splendid green grass.

She grabbed a can of cat food from the pantry shelf, put it under the can opener, and turned the machine on. Metal biting metal made a strange screech. The cats knew the sound by now; it got them excited.

Celia dumped the food into their bowl and the cats pushed each other to get to the food. Then she noticed that the red light on the answering machine was blinking. She had one message. At first she decided not to press the ON button, but she gave in.

The machine clicked. This was the message: "Celia, this is Gordon. You remember me, don't you? The union stewart. I'm sorry to bother you at—"

She hit the ERASE button. The machine whirred and erased the message.

Tomorrow, she thought, she could call in sick again. But she didn't think that was a good idea, since she needed the routine of work to take her mind off her uncle's death. Tomorrow she could deal with all of it, when she returned to work. Tomorrow the new countdown to the end of the semester also began, then she would resign and be free forever. No more teenagers. No more crazy administrators and teachers. No more homework to grade. No more lesson plans to prepare.

The cats devoured the can of food and meowed for another. She gave in and opened another can. Also, she poured a cup of dry food on the empty side of their double serving bowl.

The cats grumbled at each other.

Through the thinness of the walls came the sounds of Jane's daughter slamming doors. That kid was forever slamming doors. Celia sneezed three times. She rushed to the bathroom and blew her nose on a wad of toilet tissue. They were back, her allergies. And she knew why, too. It was a psychosomatic thing. The cats and school. Having to prepare for her classes. She wished tomorrow would never come.

Once she stopped sniffling and sneezing, she opened the medicine cabinet and reached in for the antihistamines, of which she had two kinds: mild and strong.

She opted for the strong. It would knock her out until tomorrow morning. Let it.

She cupped water with her hand and took the pill. She had exactly twenty minutes to do her lesson plans for tomorrow before the pill took effect. After that she'd not be responsible.

Changing into something more comfortable, she turned on the air-conditioner units, one in the bedroom and the other in the living room. Their humming drowned out all the other noises.

Celia sat down at the dining room table and began to plan all the days left in the week.

The phone rang. She picked it up thinking it was Rafael to tell her he was on his way.

"Celia," her mother said.

"Yes?"

"I'm calling to tell you everything's okay," she said. "I understand what you did, and I'm sorry I made you do it."

"I didn't mean to make a mess," she told her mother. "But I was furious."

"I understand," Maura said. "Things are going to change now."

In all the years, this was the first time her mother made any kind of slight acknowledgment about her drinking problem. Maybe it was a start after all.

"I am here when you need help."

"No, I intend to do it on my own."

"Are you sure?"

"Cold turkey, as the gringos call it."

"Good for you, mother."

"I just wanted to tell you."

"Thanks, I like to know how you feel."

"By the way, this Thursday I plan to cook a feast here for everybody, so tell Rafael."

"Okay."

"You are both invited."

Celia sensed a new happiness in her mother's voice, and this pleased her tremendously.

"Are you going back to work tomorrow?"

"Yes, I was sitting here preparing."

"I didn't disturb you, did I?"

"Not at all."

"I'll let you go."

"Okay."

They hung up.

The cats, who finished eating, came and jumped on the table and began the long process of bathing and cleaning themselves.

Everything would slowly return to normal; life as usual. The family dinners would resume, except that now everybody would be in town. They would stay long enough to get to know one other all over again.

Wasabi stood and came to her. He sat on her lap and fell asleep. She petted him, feeling his regular breathing.

Though the family could never recapture the years in Lomas Verdes or Havana, Celia thought, this would be a new start.

Like Wasabi, she wished she could sleep, sleep forever. Sleep until Rafael returned home and awakened her with a kiss, kiss her alive again. Such a simple thing, she thought, but why couldn't it happen in real life?

そうそ